BEING FRIENDS MEANS STICKING WITH THE TRUTH . . .

Brad had never stayed at one post long enough to have a real friend, and Alex, for some reason which Brad couldn't figure, had always been a loner. He found the answer over a campfire and a bottle of Kaluha.

"All we need," said Brad, "are two luscious babes, one for you, one for me."

Alex didn't answer.

"Who's for you?" Brad asked. "That cheerleader, Connie what's-her-name?"

Alex suddenly strapped on his pack, turned to Brad abruptly. "We never should have come on this trip. I should have told you but I couldn't."

"What the hell are you talking about?"

"I can't be your friend, Brad. If it ever comes out it's going to hurt you. People will talk behind your back, they'll make swishing gestures as you go by . . ."

"What are you saying, Alex? If I didn't know better, I'd say you were gay."

COUNTER PLAY

Bestselling SIGNET Books

☐ **FIRST STEP by Anne Snyder.** Her mother's drinking problem was ruining Cindy's life—or was she ruining things for herself. . . ? A novel about taking that all-important first step. (#W8194—$1.50)

☐ **MY NAME IS DAVY—I'M AN ALCOHOLIC by Anne Snyder.** He didn't have a friend in the world—until he discovered booze and Maxi. And suddenly the two of them were in trouble they couldn't handle, the most desperate trouble of their lives. . . . (#Y7978—$1.25)

☐ **I NEVER PROMISED YOU A ROSE GARDEN by Joanne Greenberg.** A triumphant film starring Bibi Anderson and Kathleen Quinlan based on the 5,000,000 copy bestseller. An extraordinary story about a sixteen-year-old girl who hid from life in the seductive world of madness. (#J9700—$2.25)

☐ **I WANT TO KEEP MY BABY! by Joanne Lee.** Based on the emotion-packed CBS Television Special starring Mariel Hemingway, about a teenage girl in grown-up trouble. The most emotion-wrenching experience you will ever live through . . . "It will move you, touch you, give you something to think about."—*Seattle Times* (#E9884—$1.75)

☐ **MARY JANE HARPER CRIED LAST NIGHT by Joanne Lee and T. S. Cook.** Here is a deeply moving novel and sensational CBS TV movie that brings the full horror of child abuse home. A rich, spoiled, and emotionally disturbed young mother, abandoned by her husband, takes her frustration out on her little girl . . . "Powerful, riveting, stinging, revealing!"—*Hollywood Reporter* (#E9692—$1.75)

Counter Play

Anne Snyder
and
Louis Pelletier

A SIGNET BOOK
NEW AMERICAN LIBRARY

TIMES MIRROR

PUBLISHER'S NOTE

This novel is a work of fiction. Names, characters, places, and incidents are either the product of the author's imagination or are used fictitiously, and any resemblance to actual persons, living or dead, events, or locales is entirely coincidental.

Copyright © 1981 by Anne Snyder

SIGNET TRADEMARK REG. U.S. PAT. OFF. AND FOREIGN COUNTRIES REGISTERED TRADEMARK—MARCA REGISTRADA HECHO EN CHICAGO, U.S.A.

SIGNET, SIGNET CLASSICS, MENTOR, PLUME, MERIDIAN AND NAL BOOKS are published by The New American Library, Inc., 1633 Broadway, New York, New York 10019

First Printing, August, 1981

1 2 3 4 5 6 7 8 9

PRINTED IN THE UNITED STATES OF AMERICA

counter play: A type of offensive backfield action that requires the flow to go in one direction and the ball carrier to move into the line going the opposite way.

Counter Play

Chapter One

SOMEBODY SAID THERE was a recruiter from one of the Texas colleges in the stands watching practice. Brad stood above the huddle not bothering to look. Who would cover a hick team like Fort Hanning High at the beginning of the season? Okay, we're undefeated two years running, we could have a shot at the conference title. We could also fall on our asses before the season is out. So let's play ball and forget the recruiter.

Brad checked the Blue defense. They were set for a quick rush through the middle with second and four. He smiled to himself. A college recruiter. He could just see Coach McAveety conning the guy, putting on his Woody Hayes tough-guy act, touting his winning record. God, wouldn't McAveety love to get his foot in the door of the big time, make his pitch for a college coaching spot, jump ahead to the pros, then dream himself a Ferrari and watch all those lubricious babes hanging around for extramarital excursions. Yeah, yeah, go McAveety!

The Blue defense dug in as Brad leaned down into the huddle. What if the guy wanted to talk to him? He almost laughed out loud. "And where are you heading after graduation, Bradford? I hear USC is just panting for your services." "Well, yes, sir, Mr. Recruiter, sir, the USCs are panting for my services, likewise the Yales and the Harvards, but my heart, sir, is pledged to the good old U.S. of A. I'm going to West Point where my daddy served his country, sir, and my granddaddy and my granddaddy's daddy. Yes, sir, the Academy is where I'm going."

Brad looked around at his players with a half-smile at

Alex, the flanker, and gave the signal. "Red sixty-eight, go on two."

This was the play that he and Alex had worked on over the years. He crouched behind the center, hands spread, took the ball on two, ran back, half turned, his eyes on the defense. It was sideline-and-go, Alex to run a sideline route, fake a catch, then break straight upfield. Brad made his pitch and Alex broke behind the defender. The ball flew toward the long-rehearsed meeting place. Alex was there.

BRAD STEVENS WAS one of a half-dozen army brats who had entered Fort Hanning High that September two years ago. He was fifteen then and a sophomore but already he was tall, almost six feet, muscular, with sunbaked blond hair. The army brats, children of service personnel transferred to Fort Hanning, were a little less than dirt in the high school social order. Only the tough survived the first year undamaged.

Brad liked living in a house off the post. Fort Hanning was a small town in the hills of northern California. At the turn of the century it had been a logging center where lumber fortunes had built elaborate Victorian mansions in the residential district. These homes were still there and Brad's family rented one of them. Outside of town there was a new residential section built in the boom of the twenties. But after the Great Depression, the town had quit growing. To the north there was government land where the Army had a firing range to test new weaponry.

Nothing much happened in Fort Hanning except football. That suited Brad. He didn't know too much about the game but he was a natural, and he was smart enough to know that football could open doors that would otherwise be closed. He came out for practice and nobody noticed him. The line coach put him in as tackle where the offensive team trampled him joyfully. Then he was switched to wide receiver, which wasn't his dish.

The head coach, McAveety, simply ignored him. But McAveety was a smart ball player; he knew talent when he saw it. Let the kid get his lumps. If he could take it, there would come a time when McAveety would notice him.

Brad endured. He'd been to five schools before this one; he knew the system. After ten days on the squad someone finally said "Hi" to him in the locker room. It was Alex Prager, a boy his age. He'd noticed Alex, who seemed to be a loner. Almost Brad's build, Alex was dark-skinned with a face that was saved from outright beauty by a broken nose.

One day Brad sat alone in the school cafeteria. Alex put down his tray. "This seat taken?"

"No, come on in," Brad said smiling.

That was the way it began. After a week or so Alex invited Brad to his house to listen to records. Alex had the largest collection Brad had ever seen. After they had played Neil Young and John Denver and the Led Zepplin, Alex put on a piano piece.

"What the hell is that?" Brad asked.

Alex grinned. "Mozart. You like it?"

"It's terrible."

"Listen a minute, it creeps up on you."

Brad listened. Alex left the room briefly, came back with a half bottle of wine and two glasses.

"Hey," said Brad appreciatively.

Alex filled the glasses, raised his toward Brad. "To what?" he asked.

Brad thought a second, raised his glass. "To coach McAveety, a prime shit if there ever was one."

Alex smiled. "To a prime shit."

They laughed as they drank the wine.

By October they were planning to go backpacking for Thanksgiving vacation. The regulars on the football squad were noticing the friendship by actively avoiding it. But Coach McAveety lifted the freeze when he gave Brad a shot at quarterback in practice. And McAveety wasn't the only one who watched the offensive team smooth out and work effectively with Brad calling the signals. Then Alex got a chance as flanker. It was a big day when McAveety called each of them by his first name.

That first trip, they camped in a meadow at the foot of the mountains, celebrated the end of football season with a bottle of Kaluha that Brad had liberated from his father's wine closet. The discovery of friendship was a new thing for both of them. Brad had never stayed at one post long enough to have a real friend and Alex, for some reason which Brad couldn't figure, had always been a loner.

It came out over the campfire that night at the end of the bottle of Kaluha.

Brad drained the last drop out of his tin cup, lay his head back against his pack, and looked up at the stars. "Now," he said softly, "all we need are two luscious babes, one for you, one for me."

Alex didn't answer.

"That Sally French, for instance," said Brad. "I could really accommodate Miss Sally French at this moment." He raised his head. "Right?"

"She's pretty," said Alex flatly.

"Pretty! Man, that female is the whole sexual revolution in one body."

Alex busied himself with his pack.

"Who's for you?" Brad asked. "You got your choice."

Alex shrugged, his back to Brad.

"Come on. That cheerleader with the big boobs? Connie what's-her-name?"

Alex strapped his pack, turned to Brad abruptly. "We never should have come on this trip. I shouldn't have let it get this far."

"Huh?"

"I should've told you, but I couldn't. Everything was so great with you and me."

"So it is great with you and me. What the hell are you talking about?"

"I can't be your friend, Brad. If it ever comes out, it's going to hurt you. People will talk behind your back, they'll make swishing gestures as you go by."

"If I didn't know better, I'd say you were gay."

Alex picked up his pack.

"Where are you going?"

"Back down the mountain."

"For Christ's sake sit down!"

Alex shook his head. "I *am* gay. I should have told you. I'm sorry, Brad."

Alex moved away quickly as Brad sat stunned, clasping his knees. In a moment Alex was gone.

Brad stared into the fire, the flames distorted by held-back tears. Another friendship cut off at the beginning. That was always the way. Find a new friend; move on to a new post. And now with his father in an almost permanent assignment and a friend he really liked and admired—dead end. Fifteen years old and he could count his best friends on one thumb.

He kicked the fire angrily. Goddammit, why didn't Alex keep his stupid mouth shut? Why did he have to tell me? He threw a stone into the fire.

Why? Because he's a terrific guy, you jerk, because he's the best all-around human being you ever knew. So he likes boys, so you like girls, so he likes Mozart, you like rock. What do you want? Your own reflection? He rose, picked up his pack, and carefully stomped out the fire.

He caught up with Alex as the sun was rising.

"Listen," said Brad, "what you do with your sex is your own business. You want to be my friend?"

"Of course, I want to be your friend. But I explained . . ."

"Okay, okay, you explained. Now, put down that pack and we'll have something to eat."

Alex looked closely at Brad, who returned the look steadily. He dropped the pack.

"You sure . . . ?" Alex began.

"What do you want, an affidavit?"

Alex smiled. "Okay, what's left to eat?"

"Bacon, oranges, bread, coffee."

"No more Kaluha?"

"No more Kaluha."

Brad knelt down, opened his pack, and took the lid off a cannister. The wonderful smell of coffee drifted upward as he set up breakfast for him and his friend, Alex.

That was two years ago.

THE WHISTLE BLEW for the end of practice. As the sun was coming down on the surrounding mountains, throwing long shadows in front of the stands and on the field, McAveety was standing by the bench, wide-legged, his slight potbelly and dead cigar thrust out aggressively. The bruised and tired players knew they were going to get it. It happened every year, the letdown after the big win on their first game of the season.

McAveety watched while they drifted in. They wouldn't dare flop on the grass. He'd keep them standing all through it. Seven games to go, seven wins and then a crack at the state title. He knew they could do it and he wasn't going to let the little bastards screw up his future.

He looked at Brad walking slowly, hands on hips, head down, helmet dangling from one hip. He never said it to anyone, but this kid was practically his whole team. He'd taught Brad everything, but he'd gotten it all back in two spectacular, unbeaten years, and now he felt sure he was on his way to a third. Yeah, Brad was his ticket to the big time, but by God, he wasn't going to let the kid know it.

Up in the stands, Kay Thomas and her girlfriend watched Brad and Alex shuffle toward the bench.

"There he is, number thirty-seven, next to Brad," Kay said.

"Is he cute?" Ellie asked.

"You tell me tonight."

"What's his name?"

"Alex. Alex Prager. He plays the piano like crazy."

"He's kind of sexy from the rear."

Kay laughed. "It's those tight football pants, they turn everybody on."

"What are they doing now?"

Ellie Sanders had never watched practice. She was new to Kay's group, a small redhead, kind of shy. They had invited her into the group after Drama Night. Ellie was another person onstage, all emotion and fire. The whole school knew her onstage, loved her; few of them recognized her off.

"What they are doing," Kay said, "is taking their lumps."

"I don't like Mr. McAveety. He's handsie, a toucher."

Kay nodded.

"Wasn't there some story about him and Donna Evans? I mean, she's only fifteen. Of course, she's big and looks older but . . ." She broke off, looked at Kay shyly. "We don't talk about that, do we?"

"We've got a winning team," said Kay.

Ellie understood. "But he's at least thirty."

"Thirty-two, with a wife and three kids."

Ellie was a quick study. She didn't comment.

"But he knows football," Kay said. She looked down the field. "Most of them hate him, but they know he's good at his job and he'll get them scholarships and fight the faculty to keep them eligible. And he'll do anything to get them out of trouble."

Down on the field, McAveety was in the middle of his pitch. They deserved it and they knew it. He chewed them out, one by one, not even sparing Brad, blaming him for eating the ball on a blitz when he could have thrown it away. They took the lashing in heads-down silence. And then came the end piece, the one thing Brad hated most.

McAveety stopped abruptly, looked at his downcast, abject players, then upward to the sky, then back to the players. His voice was now almost a whisper.

"Almighty God, these boys are tired; they practiced lousy; they know it. They're asking You to forgive them; they're asking for another chance this next Saturday. They'll win with Your help. Amen."

He looked fiercely at his players. They were forced to the response. "Amen," they mumbled.

McAveety walked away, a man terribly burdened by it all.

"Let's get dressed," Brad said as he and Alex walked toward the gate. He waved to Kay, who was leaving the stands. She waved back, pointed to Ellie. He nodded.

"That's your date for tonight," he said to Alex.

Alex looked up at the stands.

"Ellie Sanders. You saw her in the play."

"Oh, yeah," said Alex. "She was good."

"Kay says she's low-key."

Alex smiled. "Two of a kind, huh?"

"So play the piano, say it with music."

Alex nodded. He dated girls from time to time, always careful not to get involved. It was a form of harmless camouflage. Alex knew Brad always hoped that one of the dates would "take." Alex tried to explain. Long ago he had accepted what he was. At first, when he discovered it, he had read all the medical books, tried to change, even let himself be seduced by a female first cousin who was visiting for the weekend, but it didn't work. Then there was his friend George.

Alex was about ten or eleven when he and his friend, George, experimented, engaged in a summer of sex games. But George, counselled by his big brother, told Alex that only perverts, and queers fool around with other guys.

And abruptly, George dropped Alex, and took an exaggerated interest in girls.

Alone and terrified, Alex had recurring vivid dreams about boys. He would wake up feeling dirty, ashamed.

Then there was the Christmas vacation at Music Camp and he met a boy named Dale. His own age, Dale came from a big city, was more sophisticated. It was a loving, sweet relationship, but when camp was over, Dale went back home and Alex was alone again.

But Dale had taught him that it was okay to be what you had to be. It was better to be discreet, but never ashamed, never guilty. And finally Alex accepted what he was.

Brad and Alex went through the gate toward the gym.

"Brad . . ."

"Yeah?"

"About saying it with music. You want me to get you a couple of tickets to the concert? They're going to let me play my own composition."

"No kidding?"

"Could you make it? November tenth?"

"Try and keep me away."

"Thanks."

"For what?" Brad asked.

"For being such a great all around shit," said Alex.

Brad laughed, whacked Alex across the butt with his helmet, and they ran for the gym, tired as they were, bruised and sore as they were, but not feeling it, only feeling the joy of being such a great couple of guys, which they undoubtedly were.

Chapter Two

ON WEEK NIGHTS the squad had to get to bed early. Nobody knew who was spying for McAveety, but if you stayed out late or boozed or smoked pot or even took a friendly walk with a girl and a blanket on the golf course, McAveety knew about it. Parties broke up at ten. Play a few records, dance a little, and that's it till Saturday.

That evening, Brad wheeled the Honda out of the garage, kicked the starter of the bike, and headed for Alex's house. It was nice living off the post, feeling like a civilian. It had been a good two years, except maybe that awful bummer at the end of sophomore year.

What made him think of it was passing Sally French's house. Sally had been the "older women." Eighteen, a senior, gorgeous and ripe. He'd fallen all the way for Sally, who put a wild and wonderful end to his sexual innocence. He gloried in Sally, never a minute he wasn't thinking of her, of them, of all the delights she fashioned just for him. Oh, Sally French had it all. The trouble was she had half the football team at the same time as Brad, the budding quarterback. When Brad found out, he tried to murder the entire defensive line on every play, which cost him a broken wrist and other injuries.

McAveety knew about it but didn't drop Brad from the squad. A few knocks would do the kid good. Besides, Sally French was very easy to look at.

For months Brad shuffled around numbly. In English II he sat next to a fat girl named Kay Thomas. He didn't even know she was there. Kay was sixteen. Underneath the adolescent blubber there was a real beauty, but after her mother went off for good with her father's best friend, Kay started to eat and didn't stop.

They were a pair of disasters in row three. He didn't notice her, but she very much noticed him. One day after the bell rang, she said pointedly, "You didn't take any notes."

He was still mad at the whole world. "So what?"

And she was mad at her mother, who never even called on her birthday. "So you'll flunk the course and be ineligible and Lincoln High will walk all over us."

He turned in his seat and looked at her for the first time.

"You can copy my notes," she said.

"I don't need your notes."

She got up and left the classroom. He followed her and apologized. He did need her notes. In fact, he needed all her notes from the beginning of the semester. So they spent a number of days after class copying her notes and got to know each other. And since they were a pair of disasters, they took to eating together in the cafeteria.

One day she had her usual two desserts. Brad took the desserts and put them on another table. She looked at him defiantly. He touched her arm gently. "I'm jogging to school every morning. I'll come by your place at eight and pick you up."

She got up from the table. She was going to tell him off right then and there, but somehow what came out was, "Okay, I'll be ready."

The pounds didn't come off because she was jogging. They came off because she was totally, helplessly in love. Committed. And Brad? He felt very comfortable with her. He wasn't completely aware that she was getting prettier as the fat rolled off. All he knew was it was very good to be with Kay. And when, at the end of the year, they had become really close, it seemed as if that was the way it had always been.

Kay lived in the "new" section of town that was optimistically developed in 1927, two years before the stock market dumped the country into the Great Depression. It was a daring new concept of split levels and had what the builder called a rumpus room in the basement where the last of the "flaming youth" used to do the Charleston and raise hell on bathtub gin. In spite of all that, it was a well-built, comfortable house that carried its years without apology.

Kay's father was a contractor with long-term projects at the Fort Hanning Army base. Since her mother had left over a year ago, he had been seen with one of the attractive young secretaries at his office. It was getting serious and he had hinted at marriage. Sometimes Kay wondered wryly how she would get along with a stepmother just six years older than she. She would smile thinking about it. Would they exchange clothes, maybe? Double date, she and Brad, Norma and her father? The whole thing was absurd. But her father was a great guy and why shouldn't he have a young chick? She just hoped Norma wouldn't put him down like her mother used to.

Having a father who was dating at least three or four nights a week had advantages. He didn't always stay out late, but if he knew she was having friends over he'd beep his horn approaching the driveway just in case anything was going on that he didn't want to see.

This being Monday, there was not much going on, just a small gathering down in the rumpus room. The kids were listening to records, dancing a little, passing a joint, sipping a little wine. Very laid-back. One footballer was getting help with his geometry, obviously passing up the joint and the wine because, who knew, maybe one of the other footballers was working on the inside for McAveety.

Ellie Sanders, trying not to show it, felt lost among her new friends. She listened to the records with Alex and tried to shout conversation over the pounding beat of the latest rock group. But she was working up to one of her regular headaches. She had to excuse herself and go upstairs to the john and put a wet towel on the back of her neck. After a while she felt better, but she couldn't go back and face the noise.

There were bookshelves in the living room. She wandered in, idly scanned the titles. Kay's mother, in rebellion against small-town Fort Hanning, had formed a literary circle and the books were the only items she left after the division of the community property.

There was a set of Somerset Maugham. Ellie pulled out a familiar title.

"You like Maugham?" It was Alex, who had come upstairs wondering what had become of her.

Ellie jumped at the sound of his voice. "Oh, hello," she said. "I just couldn't take the noise."

"I know," Alex said.

"I think you and I had a stimulating conversation down there, but I couldn't hear a word of it."

Alex laughed. "Okay, we'll start a new one. Repeat. Do you like Maugham?"

She looked at the book. "He's a wonderful storyteller." She was holding *The Painted Veil*. "This is one of my favorites. Such delicious understated adultery."

Alex laughed. "You like your adultery understated."

"I do. All this bed-thrashing in modern novels is decidedly gross."

He chuckled. "You also dig subtlety."

"I certainly do." She gestured with the book. "Of course, you know that Maugham was a notorious homosexual."

Alex had been smiling. He continued smiling, controlling his face that was only imperceptibly altered.

"Yes," he said quietly, "I knew he was a homosexual. I didn't know he was notorious."

Ellie laughed lightly. "Well, they go together, don't they?"

"Could be," said Alex.

"Of course, it didn't show in his writing," Ellie went on. "At least I never noticed it."

"They conceal it well, don't they?" Alex moved a step toward the piano next to the bookshelves, touched two fingers to the keys.

"Kay says you play absolutely dreamy."

"I do," he said. "Absolutely dreamy." He sat down at the piano, opened a book of Chopin that was on the stand. "Did you know that Chopin was a notorious homosexual?" asked Alex.

"That's ridiculous. He and George Sand . . ."

"She was a notorious lesbian, everybody knew that."

Ellie laughed. "Oh, you're really putting me on, aren't you?"

Alex shook his head. "Common gossip all over Majorca."

Ellie was delighted with Alex, to find someone in Fort Hanning who could joke about the wonderful love affair of Chopin and his mistress, George Sand.

Alex began the E-flat Nocturne. At first he played mechanically, not thinking of the composition; thinking instead of why each time he met someone he really liked, it had to come to this. The cover-up, the pretending he was someone, something other than himself.

But maybe Ellie was different, he thought hopefully. Maybe it wouldn't matter. She liked him. That was obvious. They could be friends, couldn't they? He glanced at her. Her eyes were closed. She had enough sense to shut up and listen. Sure, they could be friends, why not?

Now he played with real emotion, moving away from her, letting himself go with the Nocturne.

When, a half-hour later, he lifted his hands from the keys, she couldn't say anything. She felt an overwhelming tenderness, a wanting to touch, to be touched, to hold on to a magic moment, to make whatever this wonderful thing was last forever. But Alex got up from the piano and called down to Brad that he was walking Ellie home. That put a temporary suspension on the magic moment, but offered a promise.

Ellie lived only a few blocks away, where Alex and the others had picked her up. Now she was walking home with Alex. It was a soft October night and there were pungent fallen leaves under their feet. It seemed so natural for Ellie to take his arm. And natural to glance up at the clouded moon and brush her head, just lightly, against his shoulder.

At her house, she stood in the walkway looking up at him, waiting.

Alex smiled at her. " 'Night, Ellie, see ya."

"Good night, Alex."

He started down the street. She took out her key, watching him. He broke into a jog, turned the corner, and was gone.

AFTER THE PARTY, Brad coasted the Honda toward his house, not wanting to wake up his parents. He wheeled off the street and dismounted, pushing the bike up the graveled driveway. He stopped a moment, as he often did, wondering how they had ever managed to find this fantastic house. It had been built in 1895 by a lumber king for his young bride. It was a marvel of Victorian overkill with steep gables, out-thrust turrets, wide bay windows, and a real porte cochere where elegant carriages had once delivered wasp-waisted ladies and stiff-collared gentlemen to ten-course dinners.

Brad pushed the bike through the porte cochere and past the library window. He could see his mother playing solitaire at her desk. That wasn't good. She played solitaire to quiet her nerves, and if her nerves weren't quiet, it usually meant something to do with him or his father.

Brad decided to take a walk around the block with Mug, the large mixed-breed shepherd-plus-something who was whining behind the garden gate. He parked the Honda, let Mug out, and started off.

To look at his mother was to dismiss the idea of nerves. She was tall and blond, with the same striking figure she'd had twenty years before when she married Second-Lieutenant Stevens. His father, the lieutenant, was just twenty-four, two years out of the Academy and stationed at a training base near Fayetteville, North Carolina. His mother, Katherine Ann Denning, Kitty at home, lived just outside town in an ante-bellum home with tall white columns and a large second mortgage. The Dennings were "first family," Carolina's best. All they lacked was money. Like many of their kind, they were "too poor to paint, too proud to whitewash."

Kitty could have had her pick of the presentable young men, but she fell in love with and married Lieutenant Stevens. She didn't realize she was also marrying the Army. As the years piled up, she became disenchanted with the nomadic life, the constant moves from post to post, the rootless, rigid, social order. But the Army was not disenchanted with Kitty. She was usually the most popular hostess at any station. The officers flocked around her. As a small boy, Brad remembered loud words in the upstairs bedroom after a party. Sometimes his mother was too popular with the officers and discreet transfers were arranged to another base.

Brad rounded the block. His mother was still playing solitaire. He put Mug back in the garden and opened the front door. He tried to get by to his room. " 'Night, Mom," he called.

"Brad," she said with restrained intensity.

He turned back into the library, smiled at her, and crossed to the desk to kiss the top of her head. "That better?"

"Sit down, Brad."

"Mom, it's late, I've still got some work to do."

"Please sit down," she repeated.

He sat.

"Did you know there was a gentleman from Texas College in town?"

"Yeah, someone in the locker room said he was looking for me. I got out just in time."

She smiled. "Not quite. He called here this evening. We had a nice long talk about the college. They have many advantages down there."

"Yeah, I know, Mom. I could have a car, a nice allowance, and they'd fix me up with a sleep-in roommate."

"I think that isn't funny."

"'Course it isn't, but that's the going price for football meat."

"Bradford . . ."

Her voice was edgy. She didn't use his full name unless she was upset. "The gentleman will be back tomorrow. You can at least talk to him."

"Mom, I don't want to talk to any football recruiter!" He was immediately sorry he'd raised his voice. He'd have to control himself or there would be nerves. The nerves business was something new. Ever since they'd been posted to Fort Hanning and this town that she referred to as the end of noplace. "I'm going to West Point," he said quietly. "I'm not going to play football in Texas or Ohio or anyplace else."

She looked at him, shaking her head slowly. "Darling, what kind of life is the Army? Look at your father and me. . . ."

Brad turned to go. "I've really got some work to do."

Kitty got up, put her arms around him. He could never resist her when she was loving. She raised up on her toes, kissed his cheek. "There's so much more outside the system. You could be somebody important."

He moved away from her, faked a smile. "Mom, what's the big deal? I don't have to stay in the Army after I'm through at the Academy."

"Oh, if you go, you'll stay," she said. "Your father,

your grandfather, your great-grandfather, all the ramrod gentlemen stayed. So will you."

"Hello, Bradford." His father had come downstairs, book in hand.

"Hi, Dad."

His father turned to his mother. "You're right, Kitty, all the ramrod gentlemen stayed. I hope Bradford will do the same."

Oh God, Brad thought, here we go.

His father looked at his watch. "It's late, Bradford."

"Yes, sir, I know." He hurried upstairs, calling "good night" as he ran. He closed the door to his room quickly, relieved that he didn't have to listen to it. But he could hear the murmur of their voices, subdued at first, then building to a climactic outburst and, at last, silence. Then he heard his mother running upstairs. She had taken to sleeping in one of the guest rooms since her nerves had gotten worse.

Brad undressed slowly, listening to the silence, hoping there were no aftershocks to the latest eruption. What had happened to them, his parents? He could dimly remember the times when they were happy and there was laughter in their series of homes. But then, gradually, the laughter stopped and there were the silences, the subdued anger behind closed doors.

He remembered when he was twelve, the first big blowup. They were going to be posted to Germany and his mother didn't want to go. There was almost a breakup, but suddenly there was a reconciliation. The German tour was billed as a second honeymoon and he, Brad, was left in the States with Grandpa Stevens.

Those two wonderful years with Grandpa Stevens in San Diego! Grandpa was sixty-five, looked fifty, could play like twenty and think like twelve. He had a house right on the beach. Brad learned to surf and swim almost as fast as Grandpa.

Colonel Stevens (retired) had a distinguished record

culminating, in World War II, with "conduct above and beyond the call of duty" in the Battle of the Bulge. And he had been awarded the Medal of Honor.

After Brad had lived in San Diego for two years, he realized that he was going to become a freak. And he was going to conceal it, hide it behind normal teenage behavior, but it would always be there. Grandpa's gift.

While they lived together, Grandpa shared stories of Army life dating way back in their family of soldiers. And with Grandpa, there was no apology for his way of life, there was pride, devotion to country. Oh God, Brad thought, what if you said that in the locker room today, "Devotion to Country." They'd spit in your face, call you a weirdo. And that's what he was, a freak. But nobody knew it. Not even Alex.

Brad got into bed. He wouldn't be a spit-and-polish soldier like his father, he'd be a compassionate soldier. Like Grandpa, who had read all the history books, who knew about injustice and poverty and the idiocy of war, but who knew also that some men must be around to protect what was good in their society. Freaks, like him and Grandpa.

Brad turned out the light. He had forgotten all about the book report for English IV. But it didn't matter. Kay would have all the notes he needed.

Chapter Three

EVERY DAY THAT week Ellie was in the stands watching practice with Kay. Afterward, the four of them went to the Natural Food Factory for organic salads and repulsively healthy drinks stuffed with mashed dates and other goo. The Food Factory was "in" that season and the foursome quickly established a table for themselves in the corner. The young couple who ran the place knew the dollar value of eight-week football heros. The corner table was always available.

The second game of the season was away at Lincoln High, a pushover last year with a bunch of rookie sophomores in the lineup. The betting ring headquartered in the boys' toilet at Fort Hanning High was giving Lincoln thirteen points.

Nobody could believe it when Lincoln was leading fourteen to twelve at half time.

In the visitors locker room, McAveety held back his murderous rage. He knew they had been overconfident going in. He wanted to grab every one of them and mash his face in, but he knew better. Too much was riding on this season to let his temper go. He walked between the benches where they sat, heads down, sweating sour smells of defeat.

McAveety stopped alongside Dutch Graff, the middle linebacker. "What's your problem, Graff?" he asked softly.

Dutch didn't look up. "My problem is I am getting sucked in. I'm a stupid shit."

McAveety nodded and moved on. Under the force of

his suppressed venom each of them stated his problem. McAveety made corrections in the coverage, pointed out the soft spots in Lincoln's defense. It was very controlled and rational, good, solid, fundamental football.

A minute before the end of half time he got them on their knees. Outside, the school band was playing the "fight-on" song. McAveety asked Almighty God to take over in the second half, and to infuse them all with the Divine Spirit.

Almighty God must have been listening. At the beginning of the fourth quarter, Brad threw a terrific bomb intended for Alex on the Lincoln thirty. The Lincoln safety leaped high for the pass, unable to intercept, but knocking it end over end. The ball flipped crazily into the hands of the Fort Hanning wide receiver, who had come down on the play. He raced over the Lincoln goal line standing up.

In the stands, Ellie had to put her hands over her ears to stop the sound of the insane yelling. Everybody was pounding everybody else on the back, and Kay was laughing happily at the dumb luck that had put Fort Hanning in the lead. The additional point on conversion made it Fort Hanning nineteen, Lincoln fourteen.

Fort Hanning controlled the ball for the rest of the quarter, keeping its lead intact till the clock ran out and the stands could roar onto the field and tear down the goal posts. Everybody was happy except the boys' toilet betting ring, which had given thirteen points on Lincoln.

IT WAS AFTER the Lincoln game that things began coming apart. It didn't happen all at once. But slowly, after that bad scene at the service station. Like surfers riding high on a wave, none of them saw the wipeout ahead.

Especially Alex. For the first time he could remember, he felt comfortable and safe with a girl. Ellie was just right. Not demanding, not asking anything but to be together or part of the foursome. She had a light, caressing, singing voice and Alex would play for them and often all

four would sing the corny old-fashioned songs that were
getting popular again.

One week, when Alex wrenched his knee during practice, he was given a day off. Ellie fixed a picnic lunch and
they ditched school. They went out to Green Lake and
rowed to a quiet cove. It was a hot, lazy day and after the
picnic they stretched out on the grass. They talked about
everything, finding more and more in life that they liked
and shared together. Then, after a while, they were quiet,
just lying there on the grass contentedly looking up
through the treetops.

Ellie took Alex's hand, which was alongside hers. He
knew she wanted to be kissed. Or more. Probably a lot
more. He also knew he shouldn't have come on the picnic, shouldn't have put himself, or both of them, in this
position. It wasn't that he didn't care for her. He did. She
was adorable. But.

Ellie settled it. She rolled over quickly, kissed him tenderly, shyly, lovingly. Then, when his arms didn't go
around her, she sat up, plainly hurting, and said that they
had better be going back.

But it wasn't settled for Alex. It was just the opposite.
It was what he was afraid of all the time. He was an idiot
to have thought she would be different. He should never
have started with her. He was back to the same old thing:
the covering up again . . . the acting as if . . . the pretending . . . phony smiling. He knew he had to, but still
he hated to let her go.

They gathered the picnic things and put them in the
hired boat. She sat in the stern as he pushed off. He took
the oars, facing her. His smile was so beautiful, so caring,
that Ellie read it all wrong. The way she read it, he was
shy, timid with girls, maybe even inexperienced. Well,
that could be changed. Just give it a little time; she could
wait. She smiled to herself. She was on top of that wave,
feeling she would stay there forever.

WHEN BRAD and Alex got to talking about it, they were lacing their jogging shoes in the empty locker room. Several days a week they jogged three miles from school to Alex's house, clocking it at eighteen minutes. McAveety insisted on a six-minute mile for every player on the squad.

Alex said it first. "Okay, okay, I know what you're thinking."

"All right, smart ass, what?"

"You're thinking, why didn't I do it to her. Right?"

"Look, I'm a friend, not a shrink."

"But that's what you think. Everybody does." Alex got up, jogged in place, winced as a small pain caught his bandaged knee.

"It's still bothering you?"

"A little. I'll run it out."

Brad got up, stretched, and touched his toes.

"That's what you think, isn't it? I'd be cured," Alex persisted.

"Let's run, huh?"

"And you probably think I'm a prime shit even going out with Ellie. Well I am. But she's a great girl. I really like being with her."

Brad smiled. "Welcome to Fuckupsville."

"Thanks, friend. So what's the way out?"

Brad put the stopwatch in his pocket. "Of Fuckupsville? Don't ask me. I'm a native. I've been wandering around the main drag for eighteen years."

"You? Aw, come on, Brad. . . ."

"You think you're the original mixed-up kid?"

"No, but . . ."

"Come on, let's run, work it out. Sweat's better than thinking."

They left the gym and started jogging. Brad pressed the stem of the stopwatch, ticking off the minutes to the bad scene at the service station.

AT NINE MINUTES, the elastic bandage on Alex's knee
started working loose. He nodded to a service station
across the road. "I'm going to rewind this thing and use
the can. You go ahead."

"I can stop the clock."

"No, go on. My front door's open. You can get us
something cold to drink, have it waiting."

"Okay," said Brad. He checked the stopwatch. "See
you later."

Alex held up the loose end of the elastic bandage as he
limped toward the service station. He knew the grease
monkey, a skinny little kid named Billy who was pumping
gas into a large truck. He waved as he went toward the
men's room.

"Get bit by a football?" Billy called.

"Yeah," Alex laughed.

Everybody in town knew the football players. The team
schedule was posted proudly over the service station's
cash register.

Alex entered the men's room. The hefty truck driver
was at one of the urinals. He looked Alex over. Their eyes
met for an instant.

"Hi," said the driver.

"Hi," said Alex, leaning down to the bandage.

"Joggin' huh?" said the driver.

"Yeah," said Alex.

"How far you go?"

Alex put his foot on one of the toilets, his back to the
trucker. No need to be unfriendly. "Three miles," he said.

"Pretty good," said the driver.

Alex took the metal clips off the bandage and rolled it
in reverse. He heard the urinal flush and expected to see
the trucker leaving. He continued with the bandage, then
became uncomfortably aware that the trucker was standing behind him.

Alex turned his head to see the smiling trucker standing over him. The man put his hands on Alex's shoulders, pressed gently.

"Okay, mister," said Alex quietly. "I don't need that."

"Sure you do, baby," said the trucker. "You need a little lovin'."

"Let go," said Alex, "I don't need anything."

The man pressed his groin against Alex's buttocks, tightened his grip on Alex's shoulders.

"Knock it off!" Alex yelled in fury, and swung his elbow back into the trucker's stomach. The blow pushed the trucker back. Alex grabbed the door handle, pulled the door partway open. The man lunged, threw his huge bulk against Alex.

"Billy!" Alex yelled.

The door slammed shut. The trucker grabbed Alex's sweatshirt. Alex lashed out with a backhand blow at the man's face.

"You shitty little bastard, I'll give you a little lovin'!" He drove his fist into Alex's face. Alex's head bounced against the door. Stunned, he slid to the floor.

The enraged trucker pulled Alex up, hit him again.

The door knob rattled, the door opened a crack. "What's going on here?" Billy called.

"Get the fuck outta here!" the driver yelled. No longer interested in sex, he threw his body against the door.

Billy ran to the phone in the office and called the sheriff's station.

Five minutes later Billy and the sheriff's deputy opened the door of the men's room. Alex was sitting on the floor, his face covered with blood. The trucker, still breathing heavily, was sitting on one of the toilets.

"Okay," said the deputy. "What happened?"

Alex couldn't talk.

The trucker got up. "This crummy little fag made a pass at me. I told him I didn't go for that stuff. He made a grab for my fly and I kind of went nuts and let him have it."

The deputy looked down at Alex distastefully. "What about it?"

Alex could only shake his head slowly. He wanted to say, "He's a liar, *he* made the pass at *me!*" But the words didn't come out right. The deputy helped Alex to his feet, turned to the trucker. "You want to press charges against him, mister?"

The trucker appeared to think it over. "Nah, the hell with it. He learned his lesson."

"Okay," said the deputy.

The trucker looked at his watch. "I got to get goin'. You want me to sign anything?"

"I guess not," said the deputy.

"Okay," said the trucker. He left the men's room, walked to his truck. He took his credit slip, got into the truck, and drove off.

The deputy picked up Alex's bandage. He pointed to the paper towels. "Clean up your face, sonny. I'll take you home."

On the way home, Alex realized that nobody was going to believe what had happened. He managed to talk, painfully giving his address to the deputy.

The deputy said that he had noted the trucker's license in case Alex had a different version of the incident. Alex shook his head.

As the deputy let him off he looked at Alex severely. "If I was you, sonny, I'd keep out of toilets. Know what I mean?"

Alex puked up his lunch on the sidewalk in front of his house. The deputy drove off, really disgusted with the kind of kids they were bringing up these days.

Chapter Four

BRAD CAME OUT of the front door of Alex's house on the run. "My God, what happened? Where have you been all this time?"

Alex's hands were on his knees, his head down. He retched, then lifted his bruised face.

"Oh Jeezuz," Brad said softly. He took Alex's arm gently, lifted it over his shoulder. "Come on in, we'll get some ice on that."

Leaning heavily on Brad, Alex walked unsteadily to the front door. Inside the house he sat on the edge of the bathtub as Brad brought a bowl of ice from the kitchen, wrapped the ice in a towel, and held it against Alex's jaw.

It was a long time before Alex could talk, then he told the whole sickening story.

"Oh, that sonofabitch!" Brad said, "that dirty bastard!" But he knew that there was nothing that could be done about the trucker. He held Alex's chin, moving his face gently from side to side. "Does it feel like anything's busted?"

"Uh, uh," Alex mumbled. He got up, looked at his face in the medicine cabinet mirror. "I'm okay. You can go home."

"You're not okay. I'll stay till your folks get here."

"Go home, Brad," said Alex bitterly. "Don't come back."

"Oh, we're going that route again," said Brad. "The go-away-I'm-poison pitch."

"Just go, please."

"Sit down, Alex, you need some more ice."

Alex sat down, holding his head in his hands.

Brad broke out the last tray of ice as Alex's father's car came up the driveway. Alex's father was manager of the service department of the Pontiac dealership. He was a large, powerful man, a football fanatic who could tell you the completion percentages of any passer in the NFL, who gloried in the Saturday afternoons when his boy caught the long bomb and the stands went crazy.

Alex had heard his father's car and came to the kitchen as Mr. Prager opened the door carrying a load of groceries.

Mr. Prager saw Brad first. "Bradford," he said cordially, "how's the greatest quarterback since Westy Westover?"

Brad smiled. "Fine thanks, Mr. Prager."

Then he saw Alex, who was holding the ice pack, hiding his jaw. He put down the groceries. "Son," said Mr. Prager, hurrying to Alex. He gently took the towel away from Alex's face. "Holy Mother, what hit you?"

Alex tried to smile. "I'm okay, Dad."

He touched the bruised jaw and discolored eye. "That's kind of rough football, isn't it, boy?"

"Yeah," Alex mumbled, exchanging a quick look with Brad.

Mr. Prager turned to Brad. "Maybe I ought to talk to McAveety. A game injury, that's one thing, but getting roughed up in practice. I don't like that."

"Me either," said Brad.

"Does it hurt, son?"

"I'll get by," said Alex.

"Sure you will," said Mr. Prager. He winked at Brad. "The Bums can take it, right Brad?"

"Right, Mr. Prager." Brad was very fond of Mr. Prager, proud to be one of the Bums. Ever since he met Alex two years ago, they had played touch football with Mr. Prager, the three of them calling themselves the

Bums. Most times Brad felt closer to Mr. Prager than he did to his own father.

Mr. Prager unpacked the groceries, looking at Alex's discolored eye. "Your ma isn't going to like this."

Alex nodded.

Alex's mother worked part-time at the Music Shop selling records and giving piano lessons. On the days when she worked, Mr. Prager cleaned the vegetables and got dinner started.

"She's going to raise hell, as a matter of fact." He sighed, got two potato peelers out of a drawer. "Women are funny, aren't they," he said to Brad.

"Yes, sir, they are," Brad said taking a potato peeler.

Mr. Prager laughed. "Can't live with 'em; can't live without 'em." He bubbled with the oldest clichés, but every time he came out with one it was with an air of innocent discovery. Somehow the effect was comforting, as if the unwanted clichés had found themselves a home.

Mr. Prager handed Brad a potato. They began peeling.

"You staying for supper?" he asked. "We've got plenty."

"Thanks," said Brad, "not tonight."

"I worked out a couple of good running plays this afternoon at the shop. I could show them to you."

"I'd like to, but . . ."

"It'll only take a second." He had completely forgotten Alex's injury as he took potatoes out of the bag and lined them up. "Here's our set-up, the flanker here"—he set down a potato—"the wide receiver here. . . ."

"Dad. . . ." said Alex.

"And here's the tight end. Now it's second and six . . ."

"Dad, it's Mom's car."

Mr. Prager looked out the window. "Uh, oh." He got up, crossed to the outside door, opened it. "Hiya, honey," he said.

Alex's mother was a small, dark-haired woman. You wouldn't notice her in a crowd. But when you got close enough, you found she was quite beautiful. She came in as Brad rose to greet her.

"Hello, Bradford," she said putting down her music books. Then she saw her son. "Alex!"

"Now it's okay, Grace," said Mr. Prager. "He just got roughed a little in football."

She took the ice pack away from Alex's face, drew in her breath at the ugly swelling of the jaw. Alex smiled painfully, held up his left hand, moved the fingers. "No damage, Mom, everything's okay, piano hands are fine."

She put the ice pack gently against his face. "I hate it," she said softly. "I hate that damnable game."

"Grace," said Mr. Prager, "how about I make us a couple of highballs."

"They broke his nose, they broke his collarbone. Someday they'll break his hands."

"Aw, Grace, lay off."

"He's got a concert in a month! A chance to play his own music!"

Mr. Prager took a bottle out of the cupboard. "You want soda or straight, Grace?"

"I want him to quit that brutal, stupid, senseless game before it's too late!"

"Mom, I'm okay," said Alex, trying to stop her.

"He can make it," said Brad soothingly.

She turned on Brad. "This time he'll make it. And you'll encourage him to go back and take more."

"Grace. . . ." said Mr. Prager.

She held Brad's eyes. "Why don't you let him go, Bradford! He plays the game because he admires you, he wants to be like you."

Alex got up. "Drop it, Mom! I mean it!"

She stopped. She was breathing hard but she spoke softly. "Stupid, senseless game. They teach you to cheat, to play dirty, to gouge and claw and punch. Forget the rules, just win, no matter how." She turned once more to Brad. "Let him go, Bradford, before you destroy him."

She left the kitchen quickly. Mr. Prager patted Brad on the shoulder. "She didn't mean that, Brad. She was just upset."

"It's okay," said Brad. He moved toward the door. "See you in the morning, Alex."

Alex nodded numbly. Brad closed the outside door.

Mr. Prager opened the whiskey bottle and poured himself a shot. He sat heavily at the table, downed the whiskey, picked up a potato. "I guess I better make dinner," he said.

Chapter Five

BRAD USUALLY WOKE in the morning at the sound of his father's car pulling out of the driveway. While he showered, dressed, fixed himself something to eat, he enjoyed having the big house all to himself. Kitty rarely showed before breakfast.

But today, when Brad heard his father leave for the post, he burrowed more deeply under the blankets. Something was bothering him. Oh yeah, Alex, that bad scene at the service station, that was it. He threw off the covers, sat up. No, that wasn't all of it. Mrs. Prager. He remembered exactly how she had said it. "Let him go, Bradford, before you destroy him."

He was angry at first. Me? Destroy him? That's great. And he tells me he'll destroy me. What are we, Mrs. P, a couple of werewolves? No, ma'am, we're friends, if you want to know, best friends that ever got lost in a screwed-up world. We're together, Mrs. P, not poison to each other, and together is the way we're going to be!

He felt a little better having set Mrs. Prager straight. What did she know about him and Alex? The closeness, the way they felt about each other. Reluctant to get up, he flopped back against the pillow, letting the pictures that were forming in his head have their way.

THEY WERE SIXTEEN when he and Alex went on their second fall backpacking trip. He could see both of them going down this trail in the deep woods, splashes of sunlight in the open spaces, all the damned birds in the world singing, the squirrels chattering, and Mug, Brad's large, almost shepherd mutt bounding on ahead, sniffing the underbrush, flushing a partridge and standing there, dumbfounded as the bird whirred over his head. They laughed at Mug and threw him his Frisbee. He leaped high to catch it, bouncing back to drop it at Brad's feet, seeming to say, "Okay, maybe I'm not so hot partridge-wise, but, man, you can't top me with a Frisbee."

It was a wonderful morning even though it was the first day of the hunting season and they could hear an occasional shotgun shot echo through the trees. They hadn't come to hunt, but it made it more exciting to share the forest with the hunters.

They joked about it. "You never hear the one that hits you, right soldier?" said Alex.

"What's this 'soldier' bit?" Brad asked.

"You, the West Point kid."

"Oh, yeah," said Brad.

"Hey, I hear they've got women there now."

"That's bad?"

"Do they study war like the guys?"

"Sure, they study war and English and history and languages, and you know what? Art. Just like college kids."

"No pianos?"

"Who shoots pianos?"

Alex laughed. "Brad, you really think I could make it to USC? They've got a great music department."

"You can make it anywhere if you can catch a football."

"Takes talent, huh?" said Alex grinning.

"Right. Run like hell and catch a football."

Alex broke into a fast jog. "I'm on my way."

Brad jogged along. It wasn't easy with a full pack. They were both strong and had just finished their first season as regulars. Alex was faster but Brad was tougher. Really puffing, they came to an upgrade in the trail.

Then a shotgun went off real close and Mug, who was

in a clump of bushes, let out a wild yowl and broke out running in circles.

"Jeezuz Christ!" Brad yelled. He ran to Mug, who suddenly sat down and bit at his hindquarters.

"Okay, Mug, okay," said Brad. "Let me look."

Alex ran up, dropped to one knee. "Is he hit?"

Mug was whimpering.

"It must've been bird shot, just stung him." He patted Mug. "You're all right, Mug, no blood, it's okay, boy."

Mug stood up, shook himself.

Brad got up, looked around. A big scruffy-looking kid, about sixteen, came from behind a clump of bushes. He carried an old double-barreled shotgun.

"You dumb sonofabitch!" Brad yelled at him. "You hit my dog!"

The big kid stopped. Brad and Alex moved up to him.

"Don't you look where you shoot, you stupid jerk?" Brad said angrily.

"Yeah, I look," said the kid. "I was gonna get this big rabbit and that dumb dog got in the way."

Brad looked the kid over trying to cool his anger. "You ever shoot that thing before?"

"Sure," said the kid, getting a little edgy. "I shot lotsa times, so what?"

"So you ought to have your ass whacked with it, that's what."

The kid raised the gun to a level position. "You wanna try doing it?"

"No," said Brad, "you've got the gun."

"You bet I've got the gun."

Without taking his eyes off the gun, Brad spoke to Alex. "How about Red sixty-eight, go on three?"

Alex hesitated a split second, then said, "Okay."

The kid stared at them nervously. "You spoke your piece?"

"Yeah, that's it," Brad said. Then, again watching the gun, not looking at Alex, he said, "Hut . . . hut . . ."

On the third "hut" Brad flung the gun up as Alex hit the kid with a cross-body block.

It was over in seconds. Brad broke the gun, took out the shells as the kid scrambled to his feet, gasping from the force of the block.

"You got any more shells, dump them," said Brad.

The kid emptied his pockets. Brad handed him back the gun. "Now get moving. Fast!"

The kid ran back into the woods. They laughed for minutes as they listened to him thrashing through the underbrush.

When they started along the trail again Alex said, "That was a pretty stupid move, wasn't it, with a loaded gun?"

"He had it on safety, and his fingers were off the trigger," said Brad. "I was watching those fingers."

They walked jauntily, kind of puffed up about themselves. A couple of quick thinkers, right? A couple of macho guys.

Alex thought, he's got guts, safety or no safety, and Brad thought, he's got guts throwing that block not knowing about the safety. What a pair, Prager and Stevens. Or Stevens and Prager? You name it, we got it.

They had lunch alongside a stream and then went in the icy water bare-ass. Later, twelve miles along the trail, the second thing happened. This one wasn't for laughing.

Mug was running on ahead, fresh as when they started. Every time he caught a scent he'd bounce off the trail and into the underbrush whining excitedly. Minutes later he'd come up from the rear, run past them, and do the whole thing over again.

"Look at him go," said Brad watching him disappear into the brush. "You know, when I reincarnate that's what I'm going to be, a pure-bred mutt. No problems, no stress, two squares a day, and a whole forest to pee on."

Alex laughed.

"How about you?" asked Brad.

Alex considered it. "I kind of go for dolphins."

"Intellectual type, huh?" said Brad.

"Uh, uh, show biz. Play basketball with your nose, stuff like that."

They kicked around the reincarnation fantasy for more than a mile before Brad realized that Mug hadn't brought up the rear. He clapped his hands, called the dog's name. They stopped and waited. Then, way back on the trail, they heard Mug bark, plainly calling them.

"Dumb dog," said Brad affectionately. "He's probably cornered a skunk."

They started back down the trail.

"You got any canned tomatoes in your pack?" Alex asked.

"No, why?"

"If he gets hit with skunk crud you've got to wash him in stewed tomatoes, takes out the stink."

Brad laughed, "Horseshit."

"No, that wouldn't work," said Alex. "Just tomatoes."

They laughed some more and continued back along the trail. Mug came out of a clump of tall trees, saw them, whined, and went back in. They followed.

Then they saw it. A young doe lying on the ground, her hind quarters shattered by two large-bore shotgun slugs. The ground was wet with her blood. She was plainly dying and in great pain, but making no sound, only a feeble movement of retreat as the two boys came to her.

"Oh, God," said Brad softly. "What kind of dirty bastard would do that?"

Alex shook his head sadly.

Brad looked around. "He must've shot, seen it was a doe, and just left her there."

The doe struggled feebly, gasping for breath.

"We've got to put her out of her misery," said Alex tightly.

Brad looked down at the doe, her black eyes seeming

to him to be pleading, her velvety muzzle covered with dry, white saliva.

"We can't just leave her here to suffer," said Alex.

"No," said Brad. "No, we can't. Oh, that bastard whoever he was that did it." He took a deep breath. "Yeah, we've got to put her away."

Brad unbuttoned the strap of his hunting knife, pulled it out of the sheath. Mug had been sniffing at the doe, keeping a distance, but now he came closer. "Go 'way, Mug," said Brad.

He looked down at the doe, the knife in his hand. He felt his insides churning. He gripped the knife tightly, wondering where it would hurt least, where he had to do it to get it over quickly. He knelt down to the doe. She was wheezing, struggling for breath.

"I can't do it, Alex." Alex had turned his back. He turned around as Brad got up. "I can't," said Brad.

Alex held out his hand for the knife. "I'll do it, Brad."

Silently, Brad handed him the knife.

"Meet me on the trail," said Alex.

"No, I'll stay."

"Meet me, please, it'll be easier." Alex knelt down to the doe.

Brad touched Alex's shoulder. "Come on, Mug."

Mug hesitated, then followed Brad to the trail. They walked slowly the way they had come. After about ten minutes Alex caught up with them. He handed Brad the knife.

"Thanks," said Brad.

Alex nodded.

They walked slowly up the trail each thinking about the doe and about each other. He's stronger than I am, thought Brad, more compassionate. And Alex thought, he's stronger than I am. He's strong enough to admit his weakness; I couldn't admit mine.

Oh, they were a couple of almost macho guys, weren't they? But they thought highly of each other and that's what made the miles easy and the packs lighter on that day a year ago.

BRAD YAWNED, got out of bed, and pulled his sweatshirt over his head. He looked at his rumpled hair in the mirror, combed it, examined his face. What was that face scowling about? Something was wrong there.

It was the other thing digging at the back of his mind. This was the morning, the one he'd been dreading. He wanted to crawl back in bed, but he fought it, took off the sweatshirt, reached for a dress shirt and his sport jacket, threw them on the bed.

His mood lightened a little with the shower stinging on his back. The whole thing would only take a couple of hours. He wouldn't have to speak or anything, mostly just sit there and smile a lot, shake hands, deal out the small talk. "Yes, sir, it certainly is an honor to have the congressman in our corner, sir, good for team morale." "No, sir, it's never too early to take an interest in government, sir."

Reluctantly, Brad turned off the shower, stepped out, reached for his towel.

As he dressed and put on his sport jacket, he felt depressed again, put upon, like a sulky kid going off to a party he doesn't want to attend. But he had agreed weeks ago to show up at the Rotary Club breakfast, so what was his beef?

As he rode the Honda downtown toward the Rotary Club, he wondered how he had gotten into this personal-appearance thing. West Point. Period. Of course. And West Point was worth it. Once he was accepted at the Academy, he'd never make any "appearances" again.

Van Harper, the young congressman, had agreed to sponsor Brad for the appointment. Harper had asked the Academy to open a file on the boy. Then he had requested the letters of recommendation, the school transcript,

SAT scores, even a personal essay on why Brad wanted to go to the Academy.

Brad had written a real "Ask-not-what-your-country-can-do-for-you, but-what-you-can-do-for-your-country" type essay. The kicker was, he meant every word he wrote. The essence of Grandpa Stevens had been behind him guiding his pen along the familiar way. He could just see the congressman's cynical smile when he read the letter before passing it on to the Academy. Luckily, the congressman didn't know he was dealing with a genuine, class-A freak.

But when Harper had quizzed him about the essay at their first interview, Brad had kept his cool.

"Ever think about going into politics?" the congressman had chuckled.

And Brad had not answered, but he had felt guilty, much the way he felt right now. He sighed. West Point was worth it all.

The red tape had seemed endless. But when Brad had complained, Congressman Harper intimated that his personal nomination was the one the Academy would consider most carefully . . . above all the others.

From the start, there was something in the young politician's manner that prompted Brad to doublecheck the procedure for admittance. Perhaps there was a new requirement, something Dad didn't know about. But everything Harper had told him checked out.

Brad had remained suspicious of the "eager-beaver," boy wonder. And it was almost with relief when he found out what Harper wanted from *him*. The up-and-coming young Congressman nominates the up-and-coming football player for West Point; and the up-and-coming football player endorses the up-and-coming young congressman by being seen with him at public functions. A simple "you-rub-my-back, I'll-rub-yours" transaction. Expedient, politic, nothing more.

Brad parked the Honda in back of the hall and went in

the side door. He was to meet Van Harper in the anteroom for a brief talk before the breakfast. Brad's steps quickened. The congressman had made it sound as if he had some important news regarding the appointment when he had called last night.

Congressman Van Harper was pulling a pocket comb through his hair when Brad came into the room. He turned from a wall mirror and flashed his toothpaste-ad smile at Brad, motioned him to sit down. "Be right with you," he said.

Brad sat down and watched Harper sweep his comb over his forehead to camouflage his slightly receding hairline. Suddenly, he remembered that near-scandal Harper had been involved in a while back. The opposition party had dredged up something about one of the congressman's private business deals, conflict of interest, something like that. It looked pretty bad for Harper until he effectively squelched the smear by openly admitting his involvement, making a grand announcement that he was sacrificing his holdings in the interest of public service. The young, honest, dedicated politician had come out smelling like a rose.

Harper turned to Brad. "Ready for the big time, kid?" he laughed. He looked at his watch. "Let's go."

Brad stood up. "You said you had something to tell me, congressman."

"Van, call me Van."

"You hear from the Academy . . . Van?"

Harper put a hand on Brad's shoulder, looked him straight in the eye. "The operational word here is *leaked*," he said. "Let's just say—though it's not official—that your acceptance is practically a shoo-in."

In spite of himself, Brad had to grin. What the hell, a little teamwork never hurt.

There was a knock at the door. "Press!" called a voice from the other side.

"Let's go for it, buddy," said Harper, moving to the

door. He swung it open to the blinding lights of flash cameras.

Following in the wake of the briskly walking congressman, surrounded by members of the press and his usual coterie of hangers-on, Brad tried to put down the feeling that he, too, was a genuine, one hundred percent ass-kisser. Yeah, yeah, go Brad, go!

AFTER PRACTICE, McAVEETY was looking forward to a quiet little cocktail date with the one he called his "old broad." He smiled to himself as he got in his car. Yeah, young babes were okay in the sack, but the older ones were more fun on the make, more challenge. Kind of like the difference between a simple drive through the middle of the line and a beautiful screen pass.

McAveety pulled up at the Standard station.

"Hiya, Mac," said Billy.

McAveety's long-building popularity was a constant source of inner joy. It was Fort Hanning today, who knows where tomorrow. Wherever it was, it was going to be big. A Super Bowl of a tomorrow.

"Fill her up, Mac?"

"Yeah, fill her, Billy."

McAveety got out for a visual check of the tires.

"Hey, how's Prager doing?" Billy asked.

"Huh?" said McAveety.

"Alex Prager. After that mixup yesterday."

McAveety looked puzzled.

"The clobbering he got." He nodded toward the men's room. "Right in there. With that trucker."

McAveety quickly realized that Alex's excuse for the missed practice was as phony as it looked and sounded at today's workout.

McAveety played it cool. "Oh, that clobbering. Yeah, he told me, but no details." He smiled confidentially at Billy. "It was something, huh?"

Billy laughed. "Was it something! Man, I tell you, they

were really going at it in there. I mean, that trucker was really giving it to Prager. The trucker was yelling 'The little fag, the dirty little queer made a pass at me and . . .'" Billy stopped, suddenly wondering if he had said too much.

McAveety maintained his confidential smile. "He called Prager a queer? You think he really made a pass at the trucker?"

Billy shut off the pump, screwed in the gas cap. "Well, I dunno, Mac. That's what the trucker told the sheriff's deputy. Check the oil?"

"No, it's okay." McAveety took out his wallet, handed Billy the credit card. Billy wrote up the charge, McAveety signed it.

He smiled at Billy, took two ten dollar bills out of his wallet, handed them to the boy, nodded toward the men's room. "Billy, whatever happened in there yesterday never happened, okay?"

Billy took the two tens in wonderful disbelief. "Okay, Mac, you bet!"

"You didn't see anything; you didn't hear anything."

Billy was grinning, skipping from foot to foot as if he were going to run off with this sudden fortune. "Okay, Mac, you can count on me."

"I know I can, Billy. And if I couldn't, I'd come back and beat the living shit out of you."

Billy laughed. "I didn't hear nothin'; I didn't see nothin'."

McAveety started the car. "Good-bye, Billy. Don't spend all of that on women."

Billy laughed again and waved the bills happily.

McAveety drove away from the station, looked at the dashboard clock. He'd be late for his date if he stopped at the sheriff's station and had a quiet talk with the deputy, but what the hell, the good thing about old broads was they were grateful for anything.

Chapter Six

IT WAS THE day before the Central High game. The practice had gone well, the game plan was set. The locker room was noisy, the kind of noise and horseplay that covers pre-game tension. It quieted quickly when McAveety came in looking solemn. Big things were on his mind. The biggest, an undefeated season, a winning team, and a ticket out of Fort Hanning forever. But he wasn't going to have a winner if scandal broke the team morale, if fingers of scorn were pointed at his players. He couldn't come right out with the problem, but he could sound a warning. He had wrestled with the way to do it, gotten down on his knees. God had come up with the answer.

He stepped up on the weighing scale, looked around at all of them. They quieted down. They figured it was going to be a pep talk or a chew-out.

But it wasn't either. McAveety had a book under his arm. He took it out, held it aloft. "The Holy Scripture," he said solemnly.

The collective thought was, "My God, it's a sermon!"

McAveety moved the Bible in an arc so that all could see. He allowed a long pause for complete control. He opened the Bible, seemed to look at each of them separately. "I'm going to read from the Holy Scripture, the book of Liviticus, chapter eighteen, verse twenty-two." He took a deep breath and read. "Ye shall not lie with a man as with a woman, that is an abomination."

The players waited. What the hell was this?

McAveety closed the book. " 'Ye shall not lie with a

man.' What that means is, God hates homosexuals. And I want to tell you, I'm on God's side."

He looked at their puzzled faces. "I'm not saying anyone here is a fag and I'm not saying anybody here isn't a fag. All I'm saying is, God doesn't like it and neither do I."

He got down from the weighing scales, walked slowly between the rows of benches, and was gone.

There was an explosion of epithets and obscenities after the door closed. No one noticed that Alex and Brad were quiet.

With running comment, the players shucked their uniforms. There was much towel snapping and horseplay as they went to the showers. With the steaming water splashing down on them, McAveety's sermonette began to look pretty funny.

Dutch Graff danced out of his shower and swished in front of Evans, the big guard. "Hey, lookit, I'm an abomination!"

There were whistles and catcalls as Dutch danced around Evans. "Why, dearie, that is a magnificent tool you have there."

Evans giggled. "You wanna lie with me, Dutch?"

Dutch drew himself up in mock dismay. "On the first date? Really, my dear." He minced down the line of showers. "Now I wanna say one thing to all you queers, no crotch grabbing during scrimmage."

They yelled and whistled.

"What've you got worth grabbing, Dutch?"

Dutch put his hand behind his head, threw out an imaginary pair of bosoms. "Get a load of them boobies, buster."

Alex was facing the shower wall, rinsing off the soap, when Dutch danced up to Brad. "Would you care for a bit of oral copulation, dearie?"

Brad glanced at Alex's back. "Knock it off, Dutch."

Dutch pretended to recoil. "Heavens to Betsy!" He appealed to the others. "Did you hear him?" He waved a limp wrist. "He rejected me!"

There were calls of "Shame!" "Apologize!" "Kiss and make up!"

Alex turned off his shower. Nobody noticed as he left the room.

Dutch swished back to his shower, turned to Brad, who was leaving. "Oh, you're so delicious! I could absolutely eat you alive!"

Brad picked up a soggy sneaker, threw a vicious pitch at Dutch's groin. There were howls of delight as the shot went home. Brad closed the shower room door.

THEY CAME OUT of the gym and headed across the empty football field. Alex walked head down, thinking. He stopped, looked around at the empty stands. "What if I gave them back the football suit. Shoved it in McAveety's face. What do I need with football?"

Brad was jolted. This was a little heavier than he expected. "You need football," he said.

"For what?"

Brad smiled wryly. "It builds character. Some day when you're a stinking rich composer they're going to ask you, how come? You'll say 'football.' I owe every bar of my music to those wonderful days on the gridiron."

Alex returned the smile. "You are such a big crock I can hardly believe it."

"I owe it all to football."

Alex laughed. "All right, all right, what's the answer?"

"Don't quit."

"Why?"

"It doesn't solve anything."

"So, what solves something."

"Nothing solves anything. Be yourself."

"Oh, for Christ's sake!"

"Well, what else?"

"People like me can't be themselves. The deck is stacked. I told you about the trucker. The deputy believed him. He wouldn't have believed me. I'm a queer."

"Listen, we've got a game tomorrow, we can solve that much."

They had come to the sidelines. There was a tin pail with a soggy sponge in it. Brad picked up the sponge, crouched behind an imaginary center. "Red seven, twenty-two, hut, hut . . ."

"Forget it."

Brad cocked his arm, aimed the sponge. "Run, you bastard! Go!"

Alex couldn't help it. He ran a few yards downfield, caught the dripping sponge. Brad jogged up to him, slapped him on the behind. "Let's get over to the Food Factory, we've got a couple of babes waiting."

They left the football field and walked toward the village. The fallen October leaves crunched under their feet. Students going home called "Hi" to them, seeking recognition from the star-circled footballers. When Alex didn't call back, Brad spoke for both of them. Like a blocker protecting his runner, Brad covered for Alex not knowing he was doing it.

THE NIGHT BEFORE the game Brad always felt a little edgy. Brad snapped off the vapid sitcom and shuffled through his pile of magazines. Maybe he ought to call Kay. Or go over the game plan. Or go downstairs and have a cheese sandwich. Or turn the TV back on again. Or. . . .

He stopped dead. He had been leafing idly through a copy of *People* magazine. And there it was. Right there in a group shot of a glamorous party in Malibu, California, there, right in front, looking like ten million dollars with a practically-nothing-on bathing suit and that gorgeous blond hair dripping down that fabulous body, there in al- most naked splendor was Sally French.

Brad looked a long time, then hastily read the gossipy article. There were several lines about Sally, referring to her as the exciting discovery of a very successful commer- cial photographer.

In the picture, the man next to her with an arm draped around her delicious shoulders and a creepy, possessive smile was Lyle Prescott, the one-time great lover of the silver screen. Brad vaguely remembered the gossip around school. Lyle Prescott, aged fifty-two, alcoholic, took little Sally French, aged twenty, under his wing, whatever the hell that meant, and was seeing that she made the right connections. Brad looked closer at Sally. That perfect shape, that lovely face. He shook his head slowly, won- dering at his rush of feeling.

Even now, two years later, just a picture of her and a warm excitement took hold of him. Okay, okay, she was a tramp, she made it with every guy on the squad. Always Miss Available.

He lowered the magazine to his lap, looked at himself in the mirror behind the closed door. A tramp? Miss Available? Come on, Bradford, let's level. She was bright, funny, sexy. Every minute with her was a delight. The only problem, she liked guys. What was so terrible about that?

He sighed, looked at her picture again. Sally French. He was sixteen at the time, just getting to be someone on campus. She was eighteen, the dazzling queen. Brad didn't dare even smile at her for fear of rejection. And even in his fantasies she was unattainable. So that one day in algebra when she called him by name and asked for help on a problem, he couldn't believe it.

After that, he helped her a number of times and then she asked him to come over to her place the night before midterm exams.

Unbelievable. He went to her place, rang the bell, his heart pumping as if he had been doing backfield sprints. She had told him that her folks would be out and they could be alone and really concentrate on the problems.

She opened the door with a throaty, inviting pronouncement of his name, "Bradford."

Her hair was wrapped in a towel and she was wearing a long white bathrobe. "Either you're early or I'm late," she said. "I just got out of the shower. Would it be too awful if I didn't get dressed?"

Brad could only shake his head.

"Come upstairs to my room." She stopped at the foot of the stairs. "Would you like a drink or anything?"

"No thanks."

"Me either. I think liquor spoils it, don't you?"

Brad couldn't ask "Spoils what?" as he followed her upstairs, his imagination running way ahead of him.

Her room was intimate, feminine; no banners, no rock group posters. The concession to study was a desk built along one wall. An algebra book and last year's test problems were laid out on the desk.

Sally sat at the desk, indicated a chair close by her side. She unfolded the single sheet of test problems, smiled at him. "You know, you're saving my life, don't you?"

Brad returned the smile, trying to keep his eyes off the top of the bathrobe, which opened invitingly at her slightest move.

"If I mess up algebra again this year . . ." she left the implied catastrophe hanging and tapped his shoulder lightly. "I don't know why you men are always so much better at math."

"It's easy when you catch on," said Brad, aware that it was not exactly a brilliant comeback, but excited to be included in the "you men" category.

"Well, I don't think I'll ever catch on," said Sally. She

pushed the paper a little closer to him. "Look at number one."

He read the problem, trying not to think about the total Sally French that lay just beneath the loosely wrapped bathrobe.

"Well, the way you begin," said Brad, "is to let R be the speed of the boat downstream and minus R be the speed upstream. Okay?"

She looked directly into his eyes, her lips opened a little. "Okay," she said softly.

"Then you take the sailing rate, eighteen miles per hour. Eighteen plus R equals the speed downstream."

"Oh, that's the way you start!" exclaimed Sally as if the ultimate secret of the universe had been revealed. She clasped his hand, which was hanging at his side. "I think I'm really going to get this."

"Well," said Brad, "you start the left side of the equation with eighteen plus R——"

"Maybe we ought to have some music," said Sally. "Music always helps me concentrate." With her free hand, she leaned over to a radio on the desk, flicked it on. Her other hand squeezed his. "It's the Decons, don't you love them!"

"Yeah," said Brad, "they're great," not knowing who the hell the Decons were and not caring.

Sally hummed with the music, keeping time with her fingers tapping the desk. "You know," she said with a light, happy laugh, "you're really a very exciting algebra teacher."

Ohmygod, thought Brad as he realized that the bathrobe had slipped from one leg, and his hand, held by hers, was pressing on the basic Sally French.

"Daddy wanted me to get tutored," Sally went on, "but I told him, I don't need a tutor. . . ."

Brad's heart began to pound. He was certain it was audible. Her hand was moving his just a little higher on the inside of her thigh.

"I told Daddy, I'm getting it for free." She laughed. "Oh, my, that sounds awful, doesn't it?"

Brad couldn't answer. She pressed his hand higher. She leaned forward. He could see the curve of her breast as the robe parted. Then she kissed him, a long kiss, slowly pressing his hand home.

His pulse pounded wildly during the kiss. When they broke away, she dropped the top of the bathrobe. "I guess the left side of the equation will have to wait," she said.

She let go of his hand, stood up. There it was, all there was of Sally French, the young, eager body, ready, waiting just for him.

"You won't need all those clothes," said Sally.

She walked slowly to the bed, turned back the cover, lay down. For a long moment she let him see what was waiting, then she reached up over her head and turned out the light.

Brad undressed quickly. He'd never "gone all the way" with a girl, but what he didn't know Miss Sally French taught him. Many times that night. And afterward he knew that he'd never forget it as long as he lived.

The phone rang. Brad put down the magazine still opened to Sally's picture. He kept looking at it as he picked up the receiver. It was Kay. He closed the magazine, feeling guilty. She wanted to have a party after the game, would that be all right? "Sure," he said, his mind not yet off Sally. And what are you doing? Kay wanted to know. He almost said, "I'm helping Sally French with her algebra," but he managed to talk coherently for several minutes.

He hardly heard what Kay said about the time for the party and whom she was inviting. He put down the phone, opened the magazine once more, then, after a long look, closed it and threw it into the wastebasket. He reached for the phone again. Maybe he ought to call Kay back and tell her just how terrific he thought she was. He dialed half her number and stopped. Instead, he took his jogging shoes out of the closet. He'd go a couple of miles with the dog. It might ease that pre-game tension.

Chapter Seven

THE CENTRAL HIGH rooting section was already in the stands. The Fort Hanning band was tuning up behind the gym. In the locker room the team was suiting up noisily, working up its energy, covering nervousness with banter, horseplay, and tough-guy obscenities.

Brad had just finished taping Alex's knee as McAveety came up to them. McAveety didn't know he was scowling. He wanted to keep it calm, impersonal. Without tipping off the other players, he wanted to show Alex he wasn't fooling around about the fag business. He wouldn't drop the kid. After all, Alex was a smart ball player, the Brad-to-Alex pass was part of the winning ticket. But he had to put the kid in his place, make him walk straight, stand up like a man. He looked at Alex's knee. "That bothering you?"

"No, sir, not a bit," said Alex bouncing up and down to show the flexibility of the knee.

McAveety nodded to Davis, the black flanker. "I'm starting Davis. I want to see how he does."

"Okay," said Alex quietly. Davis was his substitute.

McAveety turned to the rest of the players. "All right," he yelled, "let's get out there!" He moved quickly down the aisle of benches, the players jogging after him.

It was the first time Alex hadn't started in two seasons.

Brad picked up his helmet as Alex walked ahead. Brad caught up with him. "Maybe he is worried about your knee."

"We ran timing patterns yesterday," Alex said flatly. "He wasn't worried then."

They came out of the gym, joined the players jogging toward the stands.

"He doesn't lose games just because he doesn't like somebody," said Brad.

Alex didn't answer.

There was a wild roar as the team came out from under the stands and onto the field. Alex's father could hardly sit still. He poked Ellie. "There he is, number thirty-seven!"

Ellie laughed delightedly and felt a rush of tenderness and joy at the sight of thirty-seven gracefully catching a warmup pass.

The band filed in; the players left the field; the coin was tossed and Fort Hanning chose to receive. The Fort Hanning defensive team ran the ball back to their own forty, then the offense took over. Number thirty-seven sat on the bench. Mr. Prager was stunned. Alex always started. It was Ellie who had to figure out about the knee.

Fort Hanning was in the groove. Almost everything they did was right. At the end of the half it was Fort Hanning nineteen, Central nothing. At the end of the third quarter Fort Hanning had piled up thirty-three points. Number thirty-seven was still on the bench.

Alex tried to concentrate on the game, to be ready. Davis, his substitute, had caught three passes for good gains. Well, the hell with that, just concentrate. Try not to think about McAveety and the chapter from Leviticus; try not to think about that truck driver and about the shower room with Dutch swishing by.

"Prager." It was the assistant backfield coach standing in front of him. "You're on. Check with Mac."

Alex grabbed his helmet, ran to McAveety, who gave him instructions for Brad.

Alex ran out onto the field, Davis ran off to a rousing cheer from the stands. On the second down, Brad smiled at Alex and called for a sideline and go with Alex on the receiving end.

The ball was snapped. Brad ran back, cocked his arm, pumped a fake, then threw a long pass toward the sideline. Alex was there as the safety man was charging in. Alex turned, protecting the ball which came high and fast. He leaped up, misjudged. He held the ball for a second, then lost it. The safety man grabbed it in the air and took off. The Central blockers quickly protected their man. Incredibly, he ran it all the way for Central's only score of the game. In five more minutes of play the game was over.

ELLIE SAT VERY quietly, unseen, scrunched down in a side aisle seat of the empty auditorium. The single standing light on the stage was behind Alex and the grand piano as he played his senior composition. His mother had told him to try it on the stage, imagine an audience, get to know the piano.

It felt good, the way he was playing it. The nervousness he had projected ahead to his concert was gone. At the end of the piece, he let the whole thing hang out in a burst of fabulous sounds and a thunderous climax.

He lifted his hands, dropped them to his sides. His mother had told him how he must stand at the end and incline his head slightly to the applause. And smile, of course. He'd be damned if he'd do that now, bow and smirk to five hundred empty seats.

Then he heard it. The clapping of two hands as Ellie stepped out into the aisle.

"It was beautiful, Alex."

He turned in his seat, peered past the glare of the light to see her. "How did you get in here? The doors were supposed to be locked."

She was climbing the four steps to the stage. "I told the super I was on the concert committee. He let me in." She sat on a chair next to the piano. "Play some more, Alex."

He looked at her a long time, not turning back to the piano.

"Why haven't you called me?" she said softly.

"I've been busy."

"All week? Every day? Every night?"

"Well, yeah, I guess it has been every day."

"Oh, Alex. . . ."

"We've got an important game tomorrow, Ellie. And I had to get in a report and practice the music . . ."

"And go out the back door of the gym when you thought I was waiting in front."

"Ellie. . . ."

"What did I do, Alex?"

"Nothing, nothing."

"Something that offended you?"

"No, no. . . ."

"If I did, I didn't mean it."

"You didn't do anything."

"I must have. We were getting to be such friends, getting so close. . . ."

"Ellie, it's nothing you did, believe me."

"Then what?" She was looking at him directly, searching his face, hoping for a smile, a simple explanation.

He turned back to the piano, unable to meet her look.

She stood up, took a step toward him, and put her hands on his shoulders.

He touched her hands. "Nothing you did, Ellie."

For a long moment she held him. He stood up, turned, put his arms around her. "Ellie . . . Ellie. . . ." he said softly. He touched her hair in a gentle caress. "This never should have happened."

She looked up at him, "Please, kiss me."

He kissed her very gently, then held her at arm's length. "Could we be friends? Just friends?"

"There's someone else," said Ellie flatly. "Some other girl."

He laughed bitterly. "Oh God, no, nothing like that."

"Alex. . . ."

"If we were friends, in time you'd realize. . . ."

"I want to know now. Don't I have a right to know? If it's something I did. . . ."

Alex couldn't look at her. She did have a right to know. He'd been fighting with himself all week, avoiding her, hoping somehow she'd understand that something was wrong and forget him. What she wanted couldn't be. But how could he tell her, where were the right words? And what if he didn't tell her the truth, what if. . . .

He took a deep breath, touched a few notes on the piano. "Ellie, I can't love you in the same way as Brad and Kay love each other. I mean, you're a terrific girl, I enjoy us together. . . ."

"I'm not asking you to sleep with me, Alex. I know you're shy."

"I'm not shy. I just don't hack it with girls."

"What?"

"Girls, they're not for me."

"Alex. . . ."

"I thought maybe you'd realize. . . ."

"Realize what?"

"Do I have to spell it out? Do you remember that first date? What you said about Somerset Maugham? The word you used? Homosexual? That's me, the same as him."

She saw the pain and the tenderness in his face, the plea for understanding. "No," she said slowly, "that can't be."

"It is, Ellie."

"It isn't. You're just saying that. There is someone else, you're just making it up."

"Ellie! For God's sake! Do you think I'd make up something like that! I've been needing to tell you, wanting to tell you, I shouldn't have let it get this far. . . ."

"I love you, Alex."

They stood looking at each other. He wanted to take her in his arms again, comfort her, but he knew he'd have to cut it short right this minute.

"Alex . . . things could change. . . ."

"Nothing can change. It's too late. Nothing can ever change it, Ellie."

He jumped down from the stage and ran up the aisle without looking back. She heard the auditorium door close with a reverberating bang. The tears came slowly as she stood alone on the empty stage. Next week the poetry club would have a reading on this stage and she, Ellie Sanders, had chosen to read Elizabeth Barrett Browning. "How do I love thee? Let me count the ways."

THE GEOMETRY PROBLEM was simple enough. All Brad had to do was draw this line and connect it to that line. So why hurry? Why not call Kay and say hello? He hadn't seen her since lunch at the cafeteria. He could say "Hey, I miss you, haven't seen you since lunch," something devastating like that.

He dialed. "Hi," he said lazily doodling on the geometry book.

"Brad?" she said.

He smiled into the receiver. "What do you mean, 'Brad?' You expecting Robert Redford?"

"Brad, I was going to call you."

"I know. You miss me. It's been hours and hours."

"Have you seen Alex tonight?"

"No. What's with Alex?"

"And you haven't seen Ellie."

"Well, we did have a quickie date. . . ."

"Brad, could I talk to you?"

"What do you think you're doing now?"

"I mean seriously."

"Man to man?"

"Brad. . . ."

"Is your papa home?"

"No, but. . . ."

"I know a nifty way to talk seriously."

"Really, Brad. . . ."

"If I were Robert Redford, you wouldn't say 'Really, Robert.'"

She had to smile into her end of the receiver. "All right, you can come over."

"I can't come over, I'm doing geometry."

"Bradford!"

"I'll be there in five minutes." He lowered his voice. "If you've got any clothes on, I'll turn around and come back." He hung up the phone, closed the geometry book, and hurried downstairs.

THEY LAY ON the bed, fully clothed, but touching tenderly. She rolled over and he rubbed her back, moving lovingly from shoulders to the small curve of her spine. She sighed in appreciation.

"Bradford," she said finally.

"Quiet," he said. "Man at work."

"I'm worried, Brad."

"You sound ready to fall apart."

She rolled over and sat up.

"What's the matter?" he said. "You don't like the service?"

She got up off the bed.

"Hey, you driving me back to geometry?"

"I want to talk, Brad."

"Well, come back, we'll talk body language."

The way she looked at him told him that body language was over for the night. He sighed.

"You know something," he said, "talk ruins more relationships than infidelity."

"It's about Ellie and Alex."

"Yeah?" he said guardedly.

"You haven't seen him?"

"No. Or her. What is this?"

"Something went wrong tonight. She was in tears. She wouldn't tell me what happened. All she said was, they weren't going to see each other anymore."

He rubbed his hands down his jeans. "She didn't say why?"

"No, she kept saying 'I love him,' and then saying 'It's all over,' and then 'I love him.' "

"Maybe it's none of our business, Kay."

"But it is. Ellie's a wonderful girl and I can't see her getting hurt."

"Well, sure, and Alex is a wonderful guy . . ."

"Is he?"

"Well, of course."

"What's so wonderful about letting a girl fall in love and then dropping her dead? What's great about that?"

"Now look, we don't know the whole story."

"The story is, he's chopping her to pieces! What right has he got . . ."

"Take it easy, Kay."

"Well, I mean it. You should have seen her; she's devastated."

"Okay, okay," he said softly.

"It's not okay!" she said angrily, turning away from him. She crossed to the mirror, looked at herself, turned back to him. "You know, sometimes I think Alex is a little off base."

Brad tensed. "What do you mean, 'off base?' "

"I don't know what I mean! He's just, well . . . creepy sometimes. Socially. He hasn't got any friends, just you. He never dates unless we get somebody for him."

"Kay, maybe we'd better talk about it tomorrow."

She was wound up. She faced him angrily. "And he leans on you! Sometimes when I need you, you're not there, you're doing something with Alex. It's always you and Alex. You can't do this, you can't do that, you're busy with Alex!"

"He's my friend, Kay."

"Well, what am I?"

He stood there, helpless in the face of her anger. "I guess I'd better get back to the geometry."

Tears were beginning to fill her eyes. She turned her back. "Maybe you'd better."

He took a step toward her, touched her shoulders. She shrugged his hands off. He wanted to tell Kay everything, but he couldn't betray Alex. "Okay," he said softly. "I'll see you tomorrow."

He left the house feeling as he had never felt before. There had been some fights, but this seemed to be deeper. He knew what had happened with Alex and Ellie. Maybe he had seen it coming and turned the other way. Troubled, he got on the bike and left Kay's driveway. There wouldn't be any foursome now, Kay, Brad, Ellie, and Alex. It was bigger than that.

Chapter Eight

KITTY STEVENS HAD dressed carefully for the occasion, captured just the right, capricious mood. Like a sensitive actress, she had an inherent sense of how to present herself to evoke exactly the response she wanted . . . from women as well as men. It was simple, really. All one had to do was satisfy the image that had already been preconceived.

Brad was waiting for her as she came downstairs. He hadn't wanted to do this thing today. There was so much going around in his head. The trouble with Kay last night, the growing problem of Alex, keeping the lid on things, walking the emotional tightrope. He sighed inwardly. She's after something, he thought as he helped her on with her coat. Well, he'd go along. It was never easy to resist her. "What's up?" he asked.

She kissed him on the cheek. "You'll see. Later," she said lightly, handing him her car keys.

Kitty looked at her son while he drove the Chevy. He was so handsome, so bright, so promising. He deserved everything life had to offer. And he'd have all of it . . . if he were guided in the right direction. Or, she thought with a small sigh, steered away from the wrong direction.

They were having lunch at Le Petit Jardin, the only really good restaurant in town. Every so often she took him there to "broaden his horizons." He smiled as he turned onto the circular drive of the restaurant. How was she going to broaden him today? Or was it another pitch?

She always took the table at the picture window overlooking the garden, where she could be seen. The last of the chrysanthemums were a perfect background for the russet color of her new silk dress and her shining, pale blond hair drawn into a bun at the back of her head.

Brad ordered. Crab salad for Kitty, the trout for himself. The waiter turned to go.

"Oh, Charles," said Kitty. "We'll have a bottle of Pouilly-Fuissé, please."

"Yes, madame."

Eyebrows raised, Brad said nothing. He went through the ritual of sniffing, tasting, approving the wine, making a production of it for Kitty's sake.

Her eyes sparkled as she touched her glass to his. "To us," she toasted.

"To us."

Luncheon over, their coffee before them, Brad leaned back in his chair, relaxed, smiled into his mother's eyes.

This is the time to tell him, thought Kitty, sipping her coffee. Timing is always of prime importance. In this instance, it had been ironic, her meeting McAveety, the dull little flirtation. A stroke of fate. She couldn't be remotely interested in the crude, patently obvious lecher. The coach was not exactly her cup of tea. But, out of sheer boredom, she'd accepted a date, had dinner with him. And then, in his sly way, he had divulged that disconcerting story about Alex. She had plenty of proof that Brad was all male, but her instant response had been how this would affect Brad, his standing in the community, his brilliant future.

"Now?" Brad said.

Kitty looked up. "Now, what?" she teased.

"The surprise . . . mystery . . . wine, all this."

"I have been cruel, haven't I, keeping you in suspense so long? All right, here it is. We're going skiing . . . to Aspen . . . just you and I."

"Hey, wow! Did you say Aspen?"

"Isn't it exciting?" Kitty touched his hand. "For almost

a week, just the two of us. Oh, Brad, we'll have such fun!"

"I can't believe it! What about Dad? How'd you manage it?"

"It's all settled. Your father's on a special assignment that week anyway."

"What week? When? When do we leave?"

"The twenty-sixth, day before Thanksgiving. We'll have five glorious . . ."

Brad interrupted. "Not that weekend! Did you forget? I'm going backpacking with Alex."

"I didn't forget, dear, but . . ."

"Any other weekend, choose another one," Brad said.

"Oh, darling, I can't. Those were the only available reservations. I did try, but holiday time . . . you know."

"Guess Aspen's out, then."

Kitty laughed lightly. "You can give up backpacking for Aspen, can't you?"

"It isn't just the backpacking, Mom, you know that. It's our last semester, maybe our last chance to keep up the old tradition, Alex and me."

Still trying for lightness, Kitty said, "Surely, you've grown out of that buddy-buddy adolescent stage by now. How important is it, canceling a little jaunt with a classmate?"

"He's not just a classmate. Alex is my best friend."

"Your only friend," she said softly. Brad started to protest, but Kitty pressed on. "Brad, listen. You and Alex, you're growing up, moving in different directions. A close friendship between schoolboys is fine, only natural. But if you become dependent on each other, that could be . . . well, unhealthy."

Brad stiffened. What was she hinting at? What did she know? "What's unhealthy about us going backpacking?"

Kitty weighed her words carefully. "I'm sorry, I didn't put that quite right," she said. "I'm merely trying to spare the two of you disappointment. Don't you see, darling, by

placing an exaggerated importance on your friendship,
one of you is certain to let the other down one day. It's
inevitable."

"Let's drop it, okay?" Brad said shortly.

"Very well," Kitty said quietly. She put her credit card
on the check tray, nodded—with a serene smile—to the
waiter. But her smile failed to cover the sudden shadow
that crossed her face, the almost imperceptible droop of
her shoulders.

For a moment, Brad felt contrite, sorry for her. He'd
ruined her celebration, spoiled her big surprise. He was
tempted to give in, tell her he'd go to Aspen, the hell with
Alex and backpacking.

"The service in this place is not what it was," Kitty
said, looking around for the waiter to return her credit
card. She tapped her fingertips on the table.

Brad looked at her closely. Finger-drumming was a
sure sign of an impending case of nerves. He could almost
bet she'd go to bed early with a sick headache.

But Kitty surprised him again. Leaving the restaurant,
she flashed her sunniest smile at him. "I really hate trav-
eling during the holiday season anyway—crowds, noise,
bustle. We'll go another time."

Time. She would wait. She would be patient. This was
only the beginning, Kitty reflected. She had time.

McAveety threaded the film through the projector,
looked at the clock on Miss Porter's desk. The squad was
due in five minutes to watch a screening of last Saturday's
game. Miss Porter gladly yielded her classroom for the
screenings. She loved football and was not unaware of
Francis McAveety as an interesting male presence.

He shut the louvers on the window and sat down by
the projector. At the base of the machine was a medallion
proclaiming it a gift from the Boosters Club. He sighed
contentedly. It was easy now to raise money for team ac-
tivities; it hadn't always been so.

McAveety was considered a native of Fort Hanning, though he had not been born there. He had been born a hundred miles east in Medicine Lake, where his father sold brushes door to door. Jim McAveety, his father, was basically a lazy man, but not without a certain shrewdness. There was an ad in a magazine inviting the reader to become an ordained minister in the Church of the Divine Spirit; send eight dollars and seventy-five cents for postage and handling of the certificate of ordination. The ad also said that if the reader had a mind to spread the gospel, he could order, for fifty cents each, a paperback titled *Man of Nazareth,* which could be retailed for two dollars if the reader were properly ordained.

Francis McAveety was eleven at the time his father became a minister of the Church of the Divine Spirit. Being something of a gambler, his father bought five hundred of the paperbacks and, over the protests of his mother, who was a mousey sort given to frequent unexplained tears, piled the books and his family into the van and took off down the road.

Francis loved it on the road. It was like a picnic the whole summer long. When they got to Fort Hanning, Jim McAveety sold a paperback to a recently bereaved widow, who enjoyed it so much she ordered another copy. When his father left town almost the same time as the widow, young Francis was left with a weeping mother and three hundred copies of *Man of Nazareth*.

Francis, even then, was a very sharp kid. He had listened to his father's sales pitch sprinkled liberally with quotes from the Good Book. Over the rest of the summer he sold the three hundred paperbacks and became a conversation piece in the small town. The townspeople practically adopted him and saw to it that his mother obtained a job at the Fort Hanning National Bank.

Francis went to Fort Hanning High three years later and discovered football. Senior year he was named all-state quarterback. He got a football scholarship to a midwestern college and, on graduation, came back to Fort Hanning to wait for offers from the pros.

He was good, but not that good. He waited and waited and when there were no pro offers and there was a chance to coach Fort Hanning High, he grabbed it.

After all his hard work, after all his maneuverings, he finally had a real chance to get somewhere and a stupid little fag threatened to blow it sky-high!

The door of the classroom burst open as the squad piled in.

"All right, all right, take it easy!" he yelled at them.

They flopped into the seats with a minimum of horseplay, though there was some goosing among the defensive linemen.

They settled down and McAveety started the projector. As the film progressed, there were moans and groans at their mistakes, cheers at their successful plays; McAveety rewound certain sections, going over the errors.

Brad and Alex were seated in the back row, Alex uncomfortable, moving restlessly in his seat, knowing they would be coming to his fumble of the pass that led to Central High's only score of the game.

And there it was. The camera had caught Brad's throw, following it all the way, then picked up Alex as he turned for the catch.

The whole squad groaned as Alex missed the ball.

"For Christ's sake!" someone said.

McAveety didn't comment. He rewound the film, ran it again in slow motion. "Okay," he said into the darkness, "why did Prager blow that one?"

The voice shot out from somewhere in the middle of the room. "Because he's a goddamn queer!"

McAveety stopped the projector. He crossed to the window, slowly pulled up the shades. The players looked around at each other in silence. Nobody turned to look at Alex.

McAveety walked slowly back to the projector, picked

up a clipboard from the desk. "Defensive linemen report to coach Ellis, kickers on the field, three-fifteen, backfield sprints out on the track. That's all."

As they rose to go, he nodded to Dutch. "Hang around, Dutch, I want to talk to you."

They all filed out quietly. Alex slowed a little as he came by Dutch. Everyone had recognized Dutch's raspy voice. Alex clenched his fist, but Brad touched him on the shoulder, shoving him forward. They left the room. McAveety closed the door.

"Okay, you big-mouthed bastard. Explain that crack," said McAveety.

Dutch hung his head, but his voice was stubborn. "He's the fag I thought he was ever since you said it was somebody on the squad."

"You thought."

"More'n that. I know."

"What more?"

"My brother, you know my brother. . . ."

"Yeah, yeah, I know your brother. Which brother? You've got so goddamn many."

"Artie, the one that tends bar at Tully's Place."

"Okay, the Artie that tends bar."

"Well a lot of guys from the sheriff's office, they hang out at Tully's. . . ."

McAveety knew what was coming. That shitty little hick cop. He'd given the guy a bottle of Scotch. He should have given him fifty bucks.

"So they're arguing football and they're yellin' at each other and the deputy, he's loaded to the ears and says. . . ."

McAveety rolled his eyes to the ceiling. He should have given the bastard a hundred.

"He says 'Prager's nothing but a goddamn fag. Caught him making a pass at some guy in the can at the Standard station.' So my brother says."

"Never mind your brother!"

"Well, he said . . ."

"Never mind!"

McAveety was thinking. It was out now. What was it going to do to the team? Maybe everybody would forget it if they had a few more wins. After all, there must be other queers in a district school as large as Fort Hanning High. But it was such a dirty little story, for Christ's sake. Getting caught in a john, a piss pot! Jeezuz! That's some image. He worked on his rage, getting it under control. "Okay, I get the picture."

"My brother said, 'Why didn't you take him in for indecent exposure if he already had his whang out . . .'"

"Shut up!"

Dutch looked sullen. He could have embroidered the story indefinitely. When he first told it to Evans, he hadn't even thought of the "whang out" angle.

"Now look," said McAveety. "You and I have got only one thing to worry about. Right?"

"Yeah?"

"The team."

"Oh yeah, the team," said Dutch. "So drop him. Who needs fags? Davis is a good enough flanker."

McAveety shook his head. "It's like dropping some guy for being a Jew or something."

"He's a Jew fag?"

"Jeezuz, Dutch. . . ."

"Well, I mean . . ."

"I can't drop him because he's queer. Some jerk newspaper could pick up the story and we'd have half the guys in San Francisco coming here to demonstrate."

"Oh."

"No, what's got to happen, he's got to drop himself. He's got to find out football's not his game."

Dutch looked at McAveety. "Oh," he said. "Yeah, that's right," Dutch laughed. "It's a tough game, football."

McAveety looked at his watch. "You better get out there for the drill, Dutch."

Dutch stood up. "What about Brad? What if Brad got to him? Gave him a hint. . . ." He stopped, cocked his head. "Hey, you don't think Brad and him . . . ?"

"No!" McAveety's look was icy.

"Yeah, they're just friends. But you'd think . . ."

"Don't think. Go do your drill."

"Okay," said Dutch.

"Okay, *coach*."

"Yeah, okay, coach," said Dutch. He walked to the door, waved casually, and was gone.

McAveety cursed to himself softly, angrily jammed the switch on the projector. The frozen frame of Alex missing the catch was just visible on the daylit screen. McAveety grabbed a book off the desk and flung it at the picture. The screen clattered to the floor and the larger Alex looked back at him from the classroom wall.

Chapter Nine

EVERYTHING SEEMED THE same when Brad and Alex entered the school cafeteria: the steamy, strong smell of the dreary lunch menu; chili, tacos, and spaghetti, vainly masquerading in two or three variations. The clank and clatter of dishes, the banging of trays, the same old groans and moans of the kids over the same old, tired menu. Everything seemed the same, but it wasn't.

Brad and Alex were early. The cafeteria wasn't crowded. But it wasn't that; it was something else. Brad first noticed it in the line as they passed the salads. The servers behind the counter always had football small talk with him as he went down the line. "We going to take 'em Saturday? I'm giving eight to five on you, Brad." Stuff like that. But as he went down the line with Alex behind him, it was only "Hi, Brad," then eyes lowered, or "Gravy on that?" No small talk.

Brad and Alex sat at one of the big tables alone. Some of the other players came in, but they managed to get seats at the other end of the room.

Brad and Alex ate in silence. Brad looked around the room, then shoved his plate away. "You know, I'm going to be glad when the season's over. We'll get the hell out of here the day before Thanksgiving. Hey, what if we went all the way to Mount Denton, climbed to twelve thousand feet?"

"I'm going to skip practice," said Alex. "I want to work on the piano. Tell McAveety, will you?"

"You can't skip practice."

"I want to work on the piano," said Alex stubbornly.

"Look, three missed practices and he could drop you from the squad."

Alex shrugged. "So let him drop me. Why not?"

Brad slapped his palm on the table angrily. "Because I want you to stick!"

"Why?"

"I don't know why, dammit! I just do!"

But he did know why. He just couldn't come out with it, get up on a soap box, talk about honor and all that bull, say look, I believe a man's private life is his own business; I believe prejudice stinks; I hate cheating; I hate lying; I don't want to see a crummy bunch of red-neck jocks keep you out of football because you're different.

Alex repeated his question. "But why?"

Brad looked at him squarely, challenging. "I guess I don't like a quitter; maybe that's it." He picked up his tray, put it on the service table. Without a look back, he strode out of the cafeteria.

Alex caught up with him on the stairway to English IV. "I'm sorry, Brad."

"Forget it," said Brad.

"If you want me to hang in, I'll hang in."

"Suit yourself," said Brad, climbing briskly.

Alex kept at his side. At the door of English IV, Brad stopped. "Go work on your piano, Alex."

"Listen," said Alex, "I'll be on the field ten minutes early. We can go over my pass routes. Okay, Brad?"

"Some other time," Brad said flatly, and went in the room. Alex stood for a long time at the door. Dave Becker, the defensive tackle, came up the corridor, entered the classroom without saying hello to Alex.

THE STORY SPREAD quickly, building in detail as it flicked from tongue to tongue in the corridors, on the campus, in the boys' toilet, where imagination added more and more erotic footnotes.

It wasn't as if no one in Fort Hanning High had ever

heard of homosexuality. They had. It existed and fingers were sometimes pointed at shy or "arty" students, but this was different. This was one of the school heros, one of the invincibles, a footballer, a pass receiver like none the school had ever seen before. Sure, he was a loner, so okay. So he played the piano, so okay to that. But to get caught in the act, I mean right there, the two of them going at it in that can at the service station. I mean, man, that is too much.

Kay heard it from one of her group, who said she didn't want to tell Kay but thought it was her duty. And she didn't want to give all those awful details but honesty was just as compelling as duty. She realized that Kay was very close to Brad and Alex and she thought a long time about telling her, but the truth is the truth, and hearing it from a friend is better than from someone who didn't truly care for her. Right?

Kay's first reaction was anger. How could he do that to her, to Ellie, to Brad? She had been so fond of Alex, felt so close to him, like a sister. How dare he fool them all, violate their trust! Use them! Yes, that's right, use them! All three of them, as a cover for his . . . his deviation. After the anger, came tears. For what? Lost innocence? Because it had all been so beautiful with the four of them, Alex and Ellie enhancing her love for Brad? And now. Now what? Now sly looks in class, giggles in the cafeteria, whispers in the corridors.

"It's UNFAIR! Why didn't you tell me?"

She was sitting with Brad in her kitchen. She had called him as soon as she had heard and he was sitting across from her, sipping a cup of coffee.

"I was hoping you wouldn't hear it," he said.

"Oh, God, Brad. . . ."

"Look, Kay, this has nothing to do with you and me."

"Nothing to do with us! He was using us! You, me, Ellie. Using us to keep him in the closet!"

He put down the coffee cup. "All right, if you're going to talk complete nonsense, I'll go drink my coffee elsewhere."

He walked to the door. She rushed to him, threw her arms around him. "Brad . . . please. . . I don't know what to think. Stay. Talk to me. Hold me, Brad."

He turned, took her in his arms, stroked her hair. "It's okay, baby," he said softly. They stood there, holding on to each other.

After a while, without looking up, her tears dropping on his sweater, she said, "Brad, did you know about Alex?"

"Yeah. I knew it two years ago. When we first went backpacking."

She stepped away from him, wiping her eyes. "Two years ago?"

"Yeah."

"And all this time. . . ."

"Yeah, sure, all this time."

She dropped heavily into the chair. "Why? If you knew. . . ."

"Kay, you've known Alex almost as long as I have. He's a great human being, isn't he?"

She looked up at him. "Oh, Brad . . ."

"Well, isn't he?" Brad insisted.

"Two years. You've known all about him and never once . . ."

"Told you. Where would that get us? I make love to you, not Alex."

She fingered the coffee cup, turning it around in the saucer. She shook her head wearily. "I guess I'm tired, Brad. Maybe you'd better go; we'll talk tomorrow."

"Your father coming home?"

"I don't know, but maybe you'd better go anyway."

"Okay," he said. He kissed her on top of the head, crossed to the outside door.

"Brad. . . ."

He turned back. "Yeah?"

"Have you thought what they're going to say about . . . about Alex's best friend?"

"Sure I have. And I don't give a damn!"

He left. She waited to hear the clatter of the bike taking off, then she put her head on her arms, trying to shut it all out, but that wasn't possible. It all raced around and around inside her head. What could this do to Brad? To her? What were her friends thinking? That she was being used? That she was just a cover for something going on between Brad and Alex? She quickly pushed the idea down, but under the surface it bubbled, mixed with unanswerable questions, unpredictable futures.

Chapter Ten

IT WAS SUNDAY and Brad felt very down. He poked listlessly at the scrambled eggs he had made for himself, tried to read the Sunday paper that came every week from San Francisco. It had been Kitty's idea, as they moved from post to post, to have a big city paper to keep up with the outside world.

This morning the outside world was hardly worth it— murder, bombings, threats of war—and even the sports page hung low. Army had been beaten by the supposedly inferior Princeton. And his own Fort Hanning High had almost been upset by Sierra Union. Only that horse's ass, Dutch Graff, had saved the day by picking up a fumble on Sierra's thirty and running for a touchdown.

Sunday. Those awful Sundays at a new post when they had had to go to church. Father insisted it was part of being accepted, getting acquainted. At the time, Brad was only thirteen, but he'd had to dress up with an itchy tie and a blue suit. He didn't mind hymn singing. It was those squirmy, bottom-numbing sermons that made Sunday a day of adolescent horror. Finally, there was a point where Kitty rebelled. Coming home from church one day, there had been a subdued, tense quarrel. He trailed behind his parents, hearing pieces of it. At thirteen, he didn't quite understand how going to church had anything to do with an officer's service record. Did the Army take attendance? Maybe you didn't get promoted if you flunked church, something like that.

Brad was trying to make friends at one of those church-going posts. He had become acquainted with a sophisticated man of the world named Ronnie, who was thirteen and a half. Ronnie knew the answers.

It was at this time that Brad, in spite of church, had vague yearnings toward spirituality and some sort of communication with a Higher Power. He was fishing with Ronnie and they got pretty philosophical about it. "What do you suppose God wants you to do?" Brad asked, spearing a worm onto his hook.

"I'll tell you what God doesn't want you to do," said Ronnie, who was experimenting with cigarettes at this stage.

"What?" asked Brad.

"What God doesn't want you to do is play with yourself."

"Huh?" Brad said.

"Play with yourself. It's right there in the Bible. This guy, Onan, he cast his seed on the ground and God was sore as hell."

"What do you mean, he cast his seed?"

"Jerked off."

"Come on, that's not in the Bible."

"You want to bet?"

Brad felt uncertain, but he had to maintain his position. "Okay, a buck it's not in the Bible."

When they got home Ronnie showed him where it was. Brad had to pay off the buck in installments, but it was worth it. Ronnie knew all the sexy parts of the Bible and indoctrinated Brad. His father found Brad reading the Good Book one day and felt much better about his future.

Ronnie's father was a captain, one grade higher than Brad's, so Ronnie assumed a position of leadership. He was a skinny kid with a lot of nervous energy and a sex drive five years ahead of himself.

It was Ronnie who had suggested that they proposition Doris, one of the waitresses at the PX cafeteria. Doris was no beauty but she was sixteen, and Ronnie assured Brad that she had been *there*.

Brad didn't ask the exact nature of propositioning or where Doris had been when she had been *there*. But it all sounded pretty exciting.

Ronnie had discovered that Doris sometimes granted her favors to certain enlisted men in a troop carrier in the motor pool which was guarded by certain other enlisted men who could be persuaded, either by a share in the entertainment, or a small fee, to look the other way.

Ronnie had saved fifteen dollars to which he added five from Brad's car-washing money. Brad watched in awe as Ronnie shoved his tray in front of Doris's dessert station at the PX cafeteria, ordered a double raisin pie, and asked Doris if she could be at the motor pool that night, name her own time.

Doris almost fell apart with suppressed giggling as she looked at the skinny kid with the two raisin pies, but Ronnie stood his ground. When she finally got herself under control, he flashed the twenty one-dollar bills bound in a rubber band. Doris quit laughing. She looked around the almost empty cafeteria and quickly took the roll. As Ronnie and Brad went to their table, she left her station to count the money.

That night as Brad sat at dinner with his parents he felt that they surely must be seeing into the evil sinkhole of his mind. He was awash with anticipatory guilt. He could hardly eat. Ronnie had finally explained the nature of the coming events, the guidelines that would be used in completing the transaction. When Brad spilled his glass of milk, the symbolism was positively satanic. But his mother had only said "Clean it up, dear," which made him feel just twice as guilty.

At eight o'clock the two propositioners crossed the empty parade ground and went past the enlisted men's barracks. The motor pool was illumined by a clear, bright moon. As they walked toward the motor pool, Ronnie stopped. "I'll toss you, see who goes first."

Oh God, thought Brad, but he couldn't quit now. "Tails," he called.

It was heads and Ronnie strutted like a bantam. Brad sighed with relief.

They were challenged by the sentry, but Ronnie was prepared with a bottle of Scotch from his father's cellar. The sentry, warning them to make it fast, closed the gates of the motor pool as they went through. Doris was waiting at a certain troop carrier, a large, double-axeled truck covered with a canvas canopy. Two benches ran the length of the carrier on either side, and the now desirable Doris was sitting on one of them.

"Hi," said Doris in a low whisper.

"Hi," said Ronnie, man of the world.

Brad's heart was pounding so loud he could only grunt.

Assisted by a hand from Doris, the boys climbed up the back of the carrier. There was an awkward moment; the man of the world was uncertain of the next move. He finally said, somewhat meekly, "Do you think you might kind of take off your clothes, Doris?"

"Sure thing," said Doris. She took off her sweater, then her blouse, then, a bit more slowly, her bra. The two customers watched wide-eyed, breathing heavily. Next, she wiggled and her skirt dropped, then the slip.

"Wow," said Ronnie softly.

Then she stood in only her panties, shoes, and stockings.

Brad looked. And looked.

And then she slowly removed her panties.

And then all hell broke loose. A siren went off in the distance; floodlights lit up the motor pool turning the sheltering night into hideous day. Doris grabbed her clothes and ran forward out of the glare of the lights.

Maneuvers! Oh God Almighty, night maneuvers at a time like this! They couldn't get out of the truck without being spotted by a swarm of combat-dressed truck drivers pouring through the gates. The man of the world panicked and crawled under one of the benches. Doris was trying to wiggle back into her panties. "Get down," Brad said to Doris. "We'll jump off when they get out of the gates."

The siren quit moaning and they could hear barked commands as the drivers mounted their vehicles. The bed of the truck shook, the driver gunned the motor and slammed into gear. The bribed sentry gawked at a quick flash of Doris trying to put on her panties as the carrier went by.

Seconds later, the carrier swerved and shuddered to a stop, throwing Doris and Brad to the floor alongside Ronnie. The first helmeted soldier climbed aboard, rushed to the front.

"Holy jumping beans, lookit what we got for maneuvers!"

Trying to hide her charms and clutch her clothes at the same time, Doris kept saying, "Let me out, please!" but the soldiers, who had rehearsed this loading to twelve seconds, swept her back in.

Twelve seconds on the nose and the carrier took off. The driver couldn't understand the whoop of joy from the back of his truck. Troops engaged in war games were usually silent.

Some of the soldiers recognized Doris. "Hey, Doris, how about a little night maneuvers!"

"Let her alone, she's got a couple of boy friends."

Brad's face burned with embarrassment.

"Give her a break, fellas. Put on your panties, Doris."

Doris was trying to put on her panties, but the swaying carrier bounced her from lap to lap. After a while she gave up and decided to enjoy her sudden popularity.

So there she was with only shoes and stockings, sitting on the sergeant's lap, and then on the corporal's lap, and moving down the line of command, and nobody, including the driver up front, knew they had turned off on a wrong dirt road and were now deep in the woods approaching enemy territory.

The war games judge, in his jeep hidden in the trees, watched them go by, marking their position on the map. In ten minutes the carrier slowed as the driver and his inept navigator realized their error. The driver tried to turn around, but his hooded headlights failed to reveal a deep, sandy shoulder. They ground to a halt in the sand.

Out of the woods a lurching tank came crashing through the trees. At a hundred yards it lowered its forward gun and a splat of orange flame flashed out of the muzzle and was followed by the detonation. They were theoretically hit.

Immediately, another hidden jeep appeared. An officer wearing a judge's armband jumped out and ran to the carrier. He pointed his flashlight at the driver. "You've taken a direct hit, soldier. All personnel are dead."

"Yes, sir," said the driver.

The officer went to the rear of the carrier, flashed his light inside. "Everybody in here is dead. Get outside and wait for orders."

They filed out. And that left Doris and Brad and Ronnie alone in the truck bed. The officer's flashlight held on Doris, then on Ronnie, and finally on Brad.

"Bradford," said the officer.

Brad recognized the voice behind the flashlight. His world had come to an end. Only thirteen years old and everything was all over.

In the voice of doom he answered, "Yes, Father."

Chapter Eleven

THE SERMON WAS short and at the end of the service they sang two of the hymns that Brad really liked. He was surprised at himself for the quirky notion of coming to church on this gloomy Sunday, but it was working out okay. The black mood had lifted a little. Even the sermon was kind of relevant, the minister having established that all of us were, indeed, our brother's keepers.

As Brad came out of church, he saw Ellie. She turned onto the sidewalk in the direction of her house. He caught up with her.

"Hi," said Brad. "Going my way?"

Ellie looked up at him with a shy laugh. "I guess I am."

"Good, I'll go with you."

They walked in friendly silence a while, each thinking the same thing. Finally, Ellie spoke. "I called Alex twice this morning, but his mother said he was out."

"Jogging maybe," said Brad.

"Maybe," said Ellie.

They walked some more, then turned into a small park with a duck pond and picnic tables. Children were throwing bread to the ducks. They walked under the big redwood tree that gave the park its name.

"I read a play once," Ellie said. "An English play, about a private school. Of course they called them public schools, and this terrible bunch of little boys, who decided to boycott one of their group, wouldn't speak to him, turned away when he wanted to join them. I forgot what it was he did, but somehow he didn't conform. So they turned their backs on him. In the end he hanged himself. Just a boy. Hanged himself with a bed sheet."

"Alex is tougher than that," said Brad.

"Is he?"

"Believe me."

"Is he tough enough to go it alone?"

Brad shook his head. "No one is."

She stopped, looked up at him. He could see she was fighting tears. "He needs us, both of us, but he won't even let me talk to him."

"Maybe he wants time, Ellie."

They continued to walk, each thinking more about Alex. Then Ellie said abruptly, "Have you ever thought it would be better for you if he weren't your friend?"

Brad hesitated. She looked up, her eyes brimming now.

"Sure," said Brad. "I've thought of it. I've thought, why not drop him? Why fight it? What's it all worth? Why not let him go?"

"Will you?"

He shook his head slowly. "No. I need him as much as he needs me."

Ellie turned her face away. "Why don't you walk ahead, I'm dribbling all over."

He took her arm gently. "So dribble."

She laughed a little, dabbed at her eyes. They came out of the park, turned up her street.

"I could be his friend, too," said Ellie, "if that's the way he wanted it. I could love him and be his friend. But he's shutting me out."

"No," said Brad. "He's protecting you. He's been trying it with me for years."

They had come to her house.

"Protecting me?"

Brad nodded.

"He thinks I care what people say?"

"Don't you?"

"No! And you don't either."

"I'm not so sure about that," Brad said. "Maybe, in the real world it's just as important what people say as what they do."

"You don't believe that. Not for one minute."

"Right now, I don't know what I believe."

"I don't buy that either," said Ellie. She smiled up at him. "Thanks for walking me home."

"Thanks for letting me."

She ran quickly to the front door. He watched her go. Funny, they had been friends all this time, all four of them, and he had never really looked at her, talked to her. She was quite a girl, Ellie Sanders.

SATURDAY WAS THE day of the game with unbeaten Taft Union. The season was half over and this one could make or break it. Meeting an unbeaten team was always a psychological barrier. Get by this one and all's well, was the feeling in the squad. McAveety liked to see them psyched up, charged with that extra shot of adrenaline.

The Friday practice session was light drill, running the plays, setting the defensive patterns, no close contact.

Brad saw it the minute Alex came on the field. They were giving him the business. No friendly slaps on the ass, no go-get-him-boy, the way they were encouraging each other. They were shutting him out. Okay, let them, Brad thought. Alex can handle it.

They were in the huddle for passing drill. Brad stood over them, his hand on Alex's shoulder. He called the play, then slapped Alex on the ass and said, "Go get him, boy."

After the offensive drill the defensive team came in. They were working on a set to cover sideline passes. McAveety told Brad to run a play and let the defensive backs work on the receiver.

Brad called Alex's number as the receiver. They ran the play. Alex made a good catch over his shoulder and kept running it out, waiting to be tagged. The defensive set called for Dutch Graff at cornerback to cover the receiver. As Alex ran, Dutch came from behind and clipped him. Alex went down like a shot rabbit.

Everybody saw it. Nobody moved but Brad. With every vile word he ever heard, Brad ran and flung himself at Dutch, fists flailing.

McAveety and the line coach were there in seconds and pulled them apart. McAveety ordered Dutch off the field. Brad, breathing heavily, knelt down by Alex, who had struggled to a sitting position.

"I'm okay," said Alex.

The squad had not gathered around Alex, but stood off, watching Dutch leave the field.

Brad pulled Alex to his feet. McAveety blew his whistle calling the end of practice. He watched Alex walk around slowly, testing his leg.

"Your knee okay?" asked McAveety.

Alex flexed his knee, nodded.

"All right, go get your shower."

Alex limped slowly across the field. McAveety turned to Brad, nodded toward the bench. "Sit down."

They walked to the bench, sat down. McAveety, head down, drew imaginary plays in the grass. "I could can you for fighting, you know that."

Brad shrugged, not answering.

McAveety looked up at Alex limping across the field. "What are we going to do about him?"

"Let him play football," said Brad, holding his anger. "He's good at it."

"He's lousing up the team morale."

"Horseshit!" Brad said.

McAveety's face got red. "Look, you're talking to me, the coach. Never mind the horseshit."

"Horseshit," said Brad. "You're letting them ride him and you haven't done anything to stop it."

McAveety got redder. "I'm going to drop him from the squad. What do you think of that?"

Brad paused. "Okay, you drop him, you drop me."

"You don't mean that. You're grandstanding."

"Try me. Drop him and you've got a new quarterback tomorrow."

McAveety stood up. "All right! Go turn in your suit! Go play with your boyfriend, we don't need your kind!"

Brad picked up his helmet, quickly walked away.

"Brad!"

Brad didn't stop. McAveety ran after him, got in front of him.

"Goddammit, you stupid shit, go back there, we haven't finished talking!"

They stood there breathing at each other, neither one wanting to speak first.

"You going to let the team down?" said McAveety.

"If I stay, Alex is my flanker."

"That's blackmail."

"You named it."

"Look, son, I taught you every goddamn thing you know. . . ."

"About football." Brad nodded to the players, who stood on the field waiting. "What's going on out there isn't football."

They glared at each other. McAveety turned away. "Okay, he's your flanker. Let him make one wrong move and out he goes."

McAveety blew his whistle angrily. "All right, all right, let's not stand around here, let's get moving!"

The defense lined up again, getting themselves in the mood to stop Taft Union.

Chapter Twelve

TAFT UNION WAS tough. Big farm boys and sons of loggers. The game was on Taft Union's turf, but busloads of Fort Hanning fans had come. Fort Hanning had it all put together. The defense held Taft to one touchdown, and the offensive platoon waded in glory all afternoon. Alex Prager, Fort Hanning flanker, was the man. The visitors' stands couldn't get enough of him. "Go, Prager, go!" He caught five incredible passes and went over the Taft goal line twice. If the team hadn't hurried off the field on the final whistle, the Fort Hanning crowd might have carried Alex on its shoulders.

It was different in the locker room. The usual wild horseplay following a big win was going on at one end of the room. But down where Alex was taking off his suit it was quiet. No one came up and punched him joyfully, no one grabbed him and waltzed him around, nobody poured imaginary champagne on his head out of a coke bottle. No one said, "Man, that was football!"

When Brad could break away from the celebration at the far end, he came down to his locker next to Alex's.

"It was beautiful, Alex. They really loved you out there."

Alex smiled. "Thanks."

Brad sat down, began unlacing his shoes. "Jeez, that throw, I didn't think you were going to make it."

"You throw 'em, I catch 'em."

Brad gave him a warm, friendly slap on the back, nodded toward the celebration at the other end of the room. "Don't mind those adolescent shits down there."

Alex shrugged.

"Listen," Brad said. "Kay's having that party at her place tonight, the whole team. She's expecting you."

Alex dug into his locker, not looking at Brad. "I think I'll skip it."

"You've got to be there. You were the whole team today. If you're not there . . ."

"Maybe I'll celebrate with my own kind."

"What?"

"Never mind. It's not important. It's just . . ."

"Alex, come to the party."

Alex hesitated a moment. This was his best friend asking. "Okay," he said, "I'll be there."

IT SHOULD HAVE been the party of the year. Kay's father was away; Stubby Johnson, the black right guard, had brought his giant eighty-watt speakers. The pressure of the sound in the rumpus room was so heavy when you came downstairs, it was like taking a deep scuba dive. Willie Gomez, the safety man, had secretly dumped a large amount of vodka into the already mildly spiked punch. The party was all over the house, spilling out onto the lawn. It was almost one o'clock and the drink, noise, and animal excitement were ready to take a sexual turn in various secluded spaces and some not so secluded.

It should have been the best party, but Brad couldn't feel it, couldn't roll along with the current. He sat in Kay's kitchen with a cup of punch, not really feeling the few drinks which usually gave him an elegant high. He had wanted to feel good tonight, had waited for the high, danced, talked loud, laughed with the rest of them, but it hadn't taken hold. More drinks hadn't helped either.

It was all that stuff gnawing at the back of his head. Like this afternoon at the game: When he called Alex's number the third time, someone in the huddle had questioned the call. He set the guy straight, and Alex went over for the touchdown. But there it was. For the first time, someone had questioned his call.

If the quarterback loses the confidence of the team, if they doubt his calls, that's it. Was it an isolated incident, or would there be more? Could he hold them together for three more games, finish the season unbeaten?

That was only the small part of it. There was Alex. He had been avoiding a real, honest look at that one. Oh sure, everyone knew that Brad Stevens had a girl, was, in fact, the sex object of a couple of dozen girls all over the Fort Hanning campus. But supposing they started thinking? Maybe he was two-way? Likes girls *and* boys? Or that he was one-way, using girls for a cover. No, for God's sake, who would think that? Well, anybody, that's who. So what if they did? You know who you are, what difference does it make? What difference? Well, let's look at that, let's be up front, let's put on our Boy Scout uniform, face reality squarely. . . .

"Hi," Ellie's greeting interrupted his brooding.

He turned, smiled at her. "Hi. You couldn't take it down there either, huh?"

She held her hands to her ears. "Deafening." She looked at the big kitchen clock. "Alex's not coming, is he?"

"I guess not. He said he would but . . ." Brad shrugged.

"I think I'll go home. Tell Kay, will you?"

"Sure thing."

She left the room and he sat there by himself a moment. He knew he'd have to go downstairs again, show himself around a bit more, or Kay wouldn't like it. In a way, he was the host, since he was Kay's man and this was her party.

He got up, went to the stairway leading down to the rumpus room. The noise hit him like a solid wall. He went slowly down the stairs.

"Heyyyy . . . Brad!"

"Here he is, fellahs!"

"Come on, man, you got to see this!"

They were already rolling drunk, the three of them, Evans, Gomez, and Dutch Graff. They had a small fat vase for a football.

"We're gonna show the ladies and gen'mun how we did it this afternoon!"

They got into a huddle.

"Red sixty-eight, go on two," barked Evans.

Dutch straightened up, flicked a limp wrist at Evans. "Did you call my number, dearie?"

There was an explosion of laughter around the room. Stubby, the disc jockey, turned the volume down. This looked good.

Evans straightened up. "Well look, sweetheart, your number *is* eight, isn't it?"

Dutch put his hands over his eyes coyly. "Oh gracious, I almost forgot."

The whole crowd was laughing, nobody daring to look at Brad.

They got in the huddle again.

"Red sixty-eight, go on two."

Dutch tapped Evans on the shoulder. "If I make a touchdown, do I get a great big kiss?"

The party rocked with laughter.

They got in the huddle for the last time. Evans called the play, took the vase from Gomez, and tossed it to Dutch.

Dutch missed and the vase crashed to the floor.

"Oh, dear," said Dutch. Grinning broadly, he looked at Brad. "Do you mind, precious? I made a iddy biddy fumble."

Brad grabbed up the dipper from the punch bowl and threw the liquid square in Dutch's face. Dutch lunged, but Evans and Gomez grabbed him. They didn't care if he hit Brad; they just didn't want anything to get back to McAveety.

"You want to come outside?" Dutch grunted.

"Sure," said Brad.

"Nobody's going outside," said Evans. "Come on, Dutch."

Dutch tried to shake them off, but Evans and Gomez held on. And Dutch, like all of them, was always aware of McAveety. "Okay, let's get out of here," Dutch said. "This party stinks."

Evans let go of Dutch. The three of them left the now silent room. Stubby quickly restored the noise level with his eighty-watt monsters.

Brad sat wearily in the fat upholstered chair near the fireplace. The noise swirled around him. He closed his eyes, trying to shut it all out. Some girl pulled at his arm, asking him to dance. He smiled with eyes still closed, waved her away. The fatigue of the bruising, exciting day, the delayed effect of the liquor, all of it caught up with him. He put his head back and before he knew it, was sound asleep.

When he woke, they were all gone. Kay was sweeping up the broken vase. He looked at his watch. Two A.M. He knew he hadn't been much of a help to Kay in managing the party. He smiled at her, patted his lap. "Come on in, relax."

Kay dumped the broken pieces in the wastebasket.

"Hey, gorgeous." He beckoned to her.

She put down the broom, stood in front of him.

"Nice party," he said.

"It was a terrible party."

"Aw, come on, Kay. . . ."

Kay was plainly working up to something.

"There was lots of noise, lots of fun . . ." he began.

"He wasn't even here!" she burst out, "and he ruined it!"

"Huh?"

"Alex! He broke up the party without even coming to it!"

Brad sat up, looked around.

"They all went home after you fell asleep," she said bitterly.

"Well, look, Kay, you're not going to lay that all on Alex."

"Why not! Everything we do, you and me, he's into our lives, messing everything up!"

He got up, took her in his arms. "Baby, baby, you're going way overboard on this."

She was crying now.

"Sure," he said soothingly, "there's a problem. But we'll work it out."

She let herself be stroked. She felt close to him for the first time in weeks. He kept saying comforting things and they kissed one another, trying to settle it all in the way lovers have always settled troublesome matters.

Chapter Thirteen

As HE ALWAYS did late at night, Brad coasted the Honda when he reached his street. It was four A.M. now, no time to wake up the neighborhood, or his parents either.

There was a car parked at the curb in front of his house. He glided by and was startled to see someone asleep in the driver's seat. He coasted up the driveway, put the bike on its stand, and came back to the car.

It was Mr. Prager. Brad reached for the door just as Mr. Prager became aware of him. Mr. Prager, leaning over, opened the door. His face was drawn, anguished.

"Hello, Brad."

Brad knew something was very wrong. He got in the car.

"Hi, Mr. Prager, what's the trouble? Is it Alex?"

Mr. Prager peered at the dashboard clock. "He took his mother's car, Brad, I don't know where he is. I thought maybe you'd know."

"He wasn't at the party."

"I know, I know," said Mr. Prager. "I know he wasn't at the party. He . . . he told me why he wasn't at the party."

"Huh?"

"He . . ." Mr. Prager couldn't get the words out.

Oh God, Brad thought, how much has Alex told him? He looked at Mr. Prager, who had covered his face with his hands.

"He . . . told me about the game . . ." Mr. Prager began.

Brad couldn't follow this. "The game?"

"Today. The football game." He looked at Brad now, his expression numb, unbelieving. "He played so well, didn't he? Five completions. He was the greatest, wasn't he?"

"He sure was," said Brad helplessly.

"The best. The greatest. And they spit on him in the locker room. He told me why."

"Oh, Jeez," said Brad softly. "I'm sorry, Mr. Prager."

"He told me and . . . and I couldn't say anything, and I just sat there, and then he went out and took his mother's car. . . ." Mr. Prager stopped, drawing deep gasping breaths, his hands gripping the steering wheel. Brad put his hand on Mr. Prager's hand and held it firmly.

After a while, Mr. Prager said, "Where is he, Brad? I've got to talk to him."

"I don't know," Brad said. But then he thought back. Thought to the locker room that afternoon. "Maybe I'll celebrate with my own kind," Alex had said.

"I don't know," Brad repeated. "But we could take a chance. There's a place he might be, Mr. Prager."

KELLY'S PLACE WAS twenty miles out of town on the State Highway. It was the only gay bar between Fort Hanning and San Francisco. Good relations with the local deputies enabled it to stay open after hours and wink its eye at the age limits of its clientele. "Young gentlemen" were welcome as long as they minded their manners.

Alex had driven by the place at least four times. He was confused, upset, churning inside. He hadn't meant to tell his father, ever. But suddenly it had all come out when his father wanted to know why he wasn't going to the party, why he wasn't celebrating the victory that belonged mostly to him. He dumped the whole thing on his father, and then he couldn't stay to face it, couldn't take his father's unbelieving stare. He just grabbed his mother's car and ran with it. There had to be someone to talk to. His own kind. Wouldn't they understand?

Alex parked the car on the gravel in front of Kelly's. It looked like an ordinary roadside restaurant, a low pink stucco structure with a single oak door lit by an amber spot. In spite of the hour the parking area was filled with cars.

Alex sat for a long time fighting himself, saying go back, tell your father you love him, you didn't mean to hurt him. Tell him you're sorry.

Sorry for what? For being what you are? He looked at the door of Kelly's Place where two young men were coming out, laughing, joining arms in a friendly, pleasantly drunken walk to their car. The hell with it, Alex told himself, go in there, face whatever your future is going to be. That was the way he was putting it to himself. His future, these people, his kind.

It wasn't quite as dramatic as that. Kelly's Place was divided into three rooms. The main room, inside the door, had the dance floor and a bar behind it. On one end there was a game room with pinball machines, on the other a kind of TV lounge.

Alex looked at the dancers. Men with men. Some in leather jackets, some with tank tops, most virile, very masculine looking. A few tables of obviously straight couples, men and women, oggled the dancers, laughed somewhat furtively behind their hands, whispered, gawked.

Alex threaded his way between the dancers toward the bar. One couple bumped him. There was a laughing apology and a friendly smile. He tried to return the smile.

He sat at the bar hoping the bartender wouldn't ask for his ID, which he didn't have with him, and not knowing that Kelly's didn't have to be careful. Besides, he looked older.

"Hi," said the bartender.

"Hi," said Alex, surprised.

"Have I seen you here before?" the bartender asked.

"Uh . . . no," said Alex. He was about to say, "I've never been to a place like this," but checked himself.

"I didn't think so," said the bartender. "First drink is on the house. What'll it be?"

"Uh . . ."

"Ramos Gin Fizz is my specialty. Most of the boys like it."

"Fine," said Alex.

Alex watched the dancers in the mirror as the bartender mixed the drinks. So there they were. His kind? He was, for the moment at least, out of the closet. He was one of them. He didn't have to be someone else, someone always play acting, always hating it. . . .

"Ramos Gin Fizz." The bartender set it down in front of him with a flourish. "Learned how to make these in New Orleans," he said.

Alex took a sip. "It's good."

"Enjoy," said the bartender, and went back to his station.

The drink was very good. And strong. Alex could feel the warmth all the way down. He kept watching in the mirror. One couple was plainly embracing, scarcely moving to the music. It didn't turn him off, it didn't turn him on. A couple embracing, that's all. Natural enough. The way it was, that's all.

Alex kept watching the mirror, and without his asking there was soon another drink in front of him. The dancers moved slowly. It was disco music, but at this late hour turned down, more sensuous, much slower. Dreamy, kind of.

He didn't remember ordering the third drink, but there it was and alongside it another like it. He turned to see a short young man with long reddish hair and a sad look.

The young man smiled. "I'm Robin," he said.

Alex hesitated a second. Then: "I'm Alex."

"Glad to meet you, Alex." He took a sip of his drink. "Fred makes a lovely fizz, doesn't he?"

Alex smiled now. "I don't know, I've only had three of them."

They laughed easily.

"If you've had three, you're drunk," Robin said.

"Could be," Alex replied.

Robin nodded to the floor. "You want to dance?"

Alex hesitated. "No, thanks."

"I don't want to dance. I just thought I'd better ask you. I'd rather drink." Robin downed his drink rapidly and called the bartender. "Fred. . . ." He raised his glass. "Two more Ramoses."

They drank and at first talked small talk. And all the hurt of the afternoon, the silence at his end of the locker room, the mean looks, the sly swishing gestures, the terrible moment when he told his father, all of it was falling away. Talking to Robin was so . . . so relaxing, so natural.

Then, without really being aware of it, he was beginning to tell Robin the whole story, and Robin was nodding solemnly.

"If it wasn't for Brad," Alex was saying, "they would have dumped me off the team long ago."

"Brad?" said Robin.

"My best friend."

"Straight?"

The unfamiliar word didn't sink in at first. Then Alex realized what it meant. "Oh yes," he said, "straight."

"You're very fond of him."

"Yes, very."

"Does he know that?"

"Oh sure, he knows I admire him and . . ."

"I mean, does he really know how you feel?"

"Oh God, no. If he did . . ."

Robin touched Alex's hand gently. "Don't tell him, ever."

Alex nodded.

They drank in silence, a dark mood taking over.

"Maybe I'd better go," said Alex, not moving.

Robin sipped his drink. "I was in the closet until I was twenty," he said. "I was suffocating, hating myself, blaming my family, telling myself it was my mother loving me too much, my weak father. Sometimes it happens that way. But it wasn't that; it was just the way I was born."

Alex nodded, understanding.

"Once I came out, once I accepted myself, it was okay." He stepped down from his bar stool. "I don't think you can make it to your car. I'm going to help you."

"No, I'm all right," said Alex. He stepped down from his stool, stumbled clumsily as Robin caught him. Swaying, he clung to Robin. He didn't see Brad come in the front door.

Brad spotted him at once and wove his way quickly through the dancers to get to him.

"Alex. . . ."

Alex, still in Robin's grasp, looked up. "I gotta go home, Brad, my father'll be worried."

"It's okay, Alex, we're going home." Fred, the bartender, had come over to watch. "How much does he owe?" Brad asked.

"It's on me," Robin said. "Put it on my bill, Fred." The bartender nodded and went off.

Brad put one of Alex's arms around his shoulder, Robin took the other. They walked him unsteadily across the dance floor, bumping into the dancers. As they made it to the other side, the front door opened to admit two couples, boys and girls, obviously straights out to have a look at the gay world. Brad winced as he recognized Jane Donnelly, from Fort Hanning High. They couldn't turn away from her; it was too late.

"Well, hello," Jane said, with a knowing grin, "imagine finding you boys here."

"Hi," Brad mumbled.

Alex looked up blearily. "Gotta go home."

"We're going," Brad said.

Robin looked back at Jane and her friends after they passed them. "I hate slummers," he said.

"Yeah," Brad said. He opened the door. "I can make it now. Thanks."

"Okay," said Robin. He took Alex's arm off his shoulder, patted him on the back. "It's going to be okay, Alex. Don't worry."

Mr. Prager was standing by the car. He came forward now, opened his arms, and Alex fell heavily against him. Brad watched as Mr. Prager held his son tenderly, closely, saying comforting things the way he might have when Alex was a boy and had hurt himself. Alex clung to his father, probably not hearing the words, Brad thought, but feeling the love, the deep compassion.

Brad turned away, letting them have the moment.

Chapter Fourteen

MONDAY'S PRACTICE WAS especially tense. The story about Kelly's Place had already gone the rounds. Dutch and the defensive platoon moved aggressively around the locker room, throwing out obscenities, spitting manfully, shoving lesser players. When Alex failed to show for practice, the jokes were even more pointed. Brad had a hard time keeping his mind on the drills.

After practice, Brad looked for Alex in the auditorium, hoping to find him at the piano. The superintendent said he had just left.

Brad caught up with him outside the gym. Alex nodded but didn't speak. They walked in silence for a while.

Then Brad said, "How was it at home?"

"Rough."

"Your mother, huh?"

"Yeah, she hasn't stopped crying. I don't know if she ever will."

Brad touched Alex's shoulder sympathetically.

"She kept saying, 'What did I do? What do I do wrong?' As if she'd smoked grass or drunk too much coffee during pregnancy."

Brad smiled. "Mothers are like that."

"I really ought to get out, live someplace else."

"Go hide, huh?"

"Why not?"

"It isn't your way, that's why not."

"How the hell do you know what's my way?"

"I do, that's all."

"Bull," said Alex.

"Why weren't you at practice?" Brad asked.

"I just wasn't, that's all."

"Trying to protect me?" Brad asked.

"No."

"Liar."

"All right, I am being careful, you dumb jerk! After Saturday night, what are they going to say seeing us together? There go the fags, the two of them!"

"I don't give a damn what they say!" Brad said angrily. "You want to knuckle under, kiss ass, apologize for what you are, go ahead!"

"Aw, Brad. . . ."

"What the hell have you got to apologize for? Show up for practice, play your concert, the hell with the whole lot of them!"

"I don't want any more football."

"Oh, you don't, just like that, no more football! How the hell are you going to get to USC without football? You think your father can pay the tuition?"

"I'm only saying——"

"You're only saying a lot of self-pitying bull! You owe your father that scholarship."

"Dammit!" Alex said, "why do I have to owe everybody? Why doesn't somebody owe me sometime?"

They walked on until they came to the parking lot where Brad kept the Honda.

"You want a ride home?" Brad asked.

"No thanks, I'm running it."

"How about homework? I've got some new records, you could come to my place."

"Not tonight."

They came to the Honda. Brad pushed it off the stand, kicked the starter. The engine took with a roar, then throttled down.

"I'll see you at practice tomorrow," Brad said as he moved off.

Alex didn't answer.

Brad turned out of the parking lot without gunning the bike as he usually did. Most times he'd give it a big goose just for the hell of it, just for that wonderful surge of power that meant school was out, practice over, the road ahead free and clear.

But now he puttered along, things going around in his head. About Alex mostly. Was Alex going to let them down, go it alone after all? Brad felt vaguely angry. Would Alex leave him out in the cold, unprotected by the familiar friendship? Maybe he didn't know Alex as well as he thought. Maybe in the end there was no one you could really count on.

He went by the Food Factory and braked to a skidding stop halfway down the street. He'd completely forgotten about Kay. Blasted by an angry horn after he just missed an oncoming car, he wheeled around in the middle of the street. He came to a stop across from the Factory and sat on the bike, just looking at the front window.

He really didn't want to see Kay right now. She would have heard about Kelly's Place and they would have to have a serious talk. Kay was a great girl, but she could be an awful pain when she wanted to get down to something serious. Of course he couldn't blame her. Jane Donnelly must have given a pretty graphic replay of the whole Kelly scene. Alex drunk, his arm around Brad, the two of them staggering across the dance floor. That must've made a great picture!

Well, better get it over with and get back to normal relations. Let her speak her piece. He half smiled to himself. They couldn't settle the Alex question the way they had Saturday night. Not in the Food Factory, anyway! He almost laughed out loud. Man, that would be something else, wouldn't it?

He parked the bike, crossed the street, and opened the door of the Food Factory. Kay was sitting at their regular table with Dutch Graff, Evans, and another girl. Kay looked up as he came in, then returned to a seemingly animated exchange with Dutch.

Dutch saw Brad, grinned, and put his hand on Kay's shoulder in a proprietory way, waved for him to join them. Brad stared for a moment, then turned and left as quickly as he'd entered. He crossed the street and shoved the bike down from its stand. He kicked the starter, letting the engine roar out his anger. Kay and that idiot Dutch Graff! That was a pretty picture, wasn't it?

BRAD DIDN'T FEEL like coming downstairs for dinner, but he knew he'd have to show. The way his mother had said pointedly, "You'll be home for dinner," not a question but a statement, meant there would be a "discussion" at the dinner table.

Matters of discipline, ethics, money, and grades, or lack of them, were always discussed at dinner, mostly because it was the only time the three of them were together.

Even as he sat down Brad could feel the weight of tonight's agenda. He knew what it would be and waited for the opening gun. They had pot roast and browned potatoes, one of his favorite meals. Maybe he could divert them with small talk.

"Good roast, Mom," he offered.

Kitty smiled, said nothing.

"Gravy please, Dad."

Major Stevens passed the gravy.

They ate in silence for a few minutes. Then his father offered the opening round, small caliber. "How was practice today?"

"Pretty ragged," Brad said. "There's always a letdown after a big win."

Another half-minute of silence.

"Was Alex there?" asked Kitty.

"Huh?"

"At practice."

"Oh, Alex. No, he wasn't there. I don't know why."

The major laid down his knife and fork. "Is it possible that Alex was ashamed to show up for practice?"

"Why should he be ashamed?" said Brad, holding back his anger.

"You tell me, son."

"Jim . . ." his mother began.

"Let him tell me, Kitty. It seems there's a lot we haven't known about Alex these last two years." He turned to Brad. "I understand Alex is a homosexual. Is that correct, Bradford?"

"Yes, sir," said Brad. "That's correct."

"And since you were his very close friend . . ."

"Jim, I will not have you insinuate . . ."

"I am not insinuating, Kitty, I am asking."

"I'm his friend," said Brad. "That's all."

The major took a deep breath. "All right. How long have you known about him?"

"Since soon after I first met him."

"And you didn't see fit to tell us."

"I didn't think it was anyone else's business, sir."

"Brad!" his mother exclaimed.

"It isn't, Mother. Alex can't help what he is. He didn't learn it; he was born with it."

"I suppose that's his story, isn't it?" said the major coldly.

"No, sir, he hasn't got a story. He hates what he is, but he can't help it."

The major slammed his fist on the table, spilling a glass of water. "And so do I hate what he is!"

The water spread across the tablecloth. No one bothered to try and stop it.

"Jim, couldn't we discuss this without the theatrics?"

"Goddammit, Kitty, don't patronize me like that!"

We're off, thought Brad dismally. If only he could dissolve under the table like the water that was now trickling onto the carpet. He made a show of eating part of his potato, but it tasted like straw in his mouth.

"Bradford. . . ."

He had to look up at his father.

"Yes, sir?"

"You're aware of the implications of your friendship with Alex."

"Yes, sir, I am."

"And you understand that West Point demands certain standards not maintained in the ordinary college."

"Jim, for God's sake," said Kitty irritably, "this is not a court martial."

The major glared at his wife, turned back to Brad. "You are aware of all of this," he continued.

"Yes, sir."

Brad saw his father clench his teeth and inhale slowly. This was the big gun coming up. Brad braced himself.

"Very well," said the major. "I will not discuss Alex any further. I am going to give you a direct order. You are to drop Alex as a friend as of this moment. I repeat, that is a direct order."

Kitty's face flushed. She pushed back her chair. "Jim," she said angrily, "Brad is not one of your enlisted men. You do not give Brad a direct order."

"Mom . . ."

"I'm sick of it," his mother said. "This is supposed to be a family, not a military component."

"Are you through, Kitty?"

"No, I am not. I am not through at all."

"May I be excused?" asked Brad.

"I am thoroughly tired of being on the other end of the orders," Kitty said. "For twenty years I have taken orders . . ."

"Which you ignore and go your own damned way, neglecting your home, ignoring your duties . . ."

"What duties do I ignore! I've spent years entertaining an army of dull wives so that you could get your next promotion, listening to all those dull husbands . . ."

"Some of those husbands weren't so dull. Duke Ellis for one."

"That was fifteen years ago."

They didn't even know Brad was there now.

"Not only Duke, but Captain Colter, he wasn't dull, was he?"

"No, he wasn't! He was alive, interested in something beside artillery and spit-and-polish politics."

Brad got up from the table. "I've got homework."

"Jim, I've been doing a lot of thinking . . ."

" 'Night, Mom, 'night, Dad."

"So have I," said Major Stevens.

Brad got out of the dining room quickly. As he took the first steps of the old, darkly polished wooden stairway he caught one word that his mother spoke. One word that sounded like *divorce*. He stopped, listened. But their voices were subdued now, low and tense. He strained to hear the word again, came down a step, but it wasn't repeated. Maybe he hadn't heard it, maybe the word wasn't *divorce*. But it was, he knew it was.

He continued up the stairs. It was his fault really. All he had had to say was "Yes, father, I'll drop him," that's all, obey the direct order and the discussion would have ended, they wouldn't have fought. His mother wouldn't have said the word *divorce*. Well, maybe she would have. But if they had been a normal family, not Army people, not rootless wanderers from post to post. . . .

He closed the door of his room, picked up his book of irregular French verbs, opened it, snapped it shut, flung it across the room. Was it worth it, all this hassle over Alex? Was the whole thing really worth it?

ALEX SHOWED UP for practice on Tuesday but both he and Brad avoided each other as much as possible without being obvious. McAveety noticed the lack of coordination between them on the passing drills. After practice, he dismissed the squad, asked Brad and Alex to come to the bench.

They stood in front of him, waiting, rubbing off the sweat, uncomfortable in the perimeter of his displeasure. He let them hang there as long as possible. Brad could have spoken first, offered an explanation for their ragged play, but he felt an urge to stubborn resistance. Let him say it, why make it easier?

But McAveety didn't have their ragged play in mind at all. It was something else, something he had to get off his chest.

"Okay," he said abruptly, "I want to say one thing first. I don't give a damn what you two do with your private parts, that's your own business. But I do care about your football team, and that team doesn't like the way things are going. Do you read me?"

They were silent.

"That business at Kelly's Place. Every goddamn player on the team knows you two were boozing it up in a fag joint on Saturday night. And those players don't like it one goddamn bit because that reflects on them. Do you read that?"

Brad glanced at Alex. He waited for Alex to explain it. He didn't give a damn about McAveety's opinion, but a little less friction between coach and quarterback would make it easier for everyone. Alex seemed about to speak but then said nothing, looked down at a scraped knuckle, rubbed it nervously.

"Okay, you read that," said McAveety. "Now, I could send you guys up to the front office and maybe they'd suspend the both of you. But I'm not going to do that. What I'm going to do is tell you just one thing. We got three games to go and we're going to win those games with God's help. But God's going to drop us like a hot potato if we go and break his commandments."

Brad watched Alex's hand rubbing the knuckle. Why didn't he say something, ease things a little?

"God didn't write his commandments just for the hell of it," the coach went on. "He was thinking of you and me and what's good for all of us."

McAveety paused and looked directly at Alex, as though forcing Alex to raise his head and face his angry, gray-blue eyes. "If I was somebody in your spot, Prager, I'd be thinking of somebody besides myself. I'd be thinking of what's good for the team. Okay, that's all, go take your showers."

They walked slowly across the field, not looking back at McAveety sitting alone on the bench, his shoulders hunched over, his lips still moving in some silent, angry discourse.

Brad glanced at Alex. In all the two years of their friendship there had never been a time he could remember when they hadn't felt good about each other or when it wasn't the two of them together bucking a hostile world. There had never been rivalry or envy or any of the usual hassles between friends, none of that.

But now this. Alex could have said something, anything, Brad thought.

"What?" said Alex.

Brad hadn't realized he had spoken. "Nothing. I just said you could have opened your mouth back there."

"To McAveety?"

"Yeah, to McAveety. Tell him off. Anything. What right has he got to . . ."

"I thought you always said we don't need to explain things."

"Well it's better than just standing there, isn't it?"

"Hey, take it easy. This is me, your friend, Alex."

"I know, I know," Brad said.

"I mean, I could tell him off, sure. And he could kick me off the squad. And you're telling me to stick with it, I owe it to Dad. . . ."

"All right, all right. Forget it."

"I mean, I could've told McAveety about Saturday, I was going to."

"You were going to. . . ."

"Well I was, dammit!"

They stopped in front of the stands, looking angrily at each other.

"I was going to tell him," Alex said. "But I thought, why? We know where we're at, Brad and me, we don't have to explain anything to anybody. I was wrong, huh?"

Brad turned abruptly, walked through the aisle under the stands toward the gym. He was angry and confused. He was right, sure he was. But he was not too sure. I mean, Alex is my friend, okay, but why do I have to carry both of us? Why dump it all on me? Dammit, was *I* the one who should have said it?

Watching Brad go, Alex had a sick, knotted feeling in his gut, a feeling that his whole fragile world was ready to fall apart. He had built too much on Brad, he knew that, but he knew he couldn't help it, that's the way it was and always would be. He walked toward the gym, head down, helmet dragging the ground, trying to stop the agony of thinking.

Chapter Fifteen

BY THE NEXT day it almost seemed as though nothing had happened between them. Of course, Brad couldn't make it to jog home; he had a game-plan meeting with McAveety. And Alex couldn't have Brad over to listen to records because he promised his Dad he'd shoot a little pool. But it was all okay on the outside.

After practice on Friday, Brad heard something that was pretty exciting and made him stop thinking for a while about Alex and their problem. He was coming off the field toward the stands when a woman he'd never seen before got up from the front row of seats. Jerry Fergus, a third-stringer, was standing in front of her. Jerry pointed to Brad. The woman nodded, left the stands, and came toward him.

She wasn't a local person. Her outfit was too chic, too well put together. She had a cigarette in one hand, a large purse slung over one shoulder. She was small, probably in her mid-thirties, with short brown hair, a disarming smile, and a freckled face that just escaped being ugly.

"Brad Stevens?" she asked.

"That's right," Brad said.

She held out her hand. "I'm Vida Decker, *Everybody* magazine. I'd like to talk to you for a few minutes."

"Sure," said Brad. "What about? What did I do wrong?"

She laughed. "Nothing yet. Anyplace we could go for a cup of coffee?"

"The cafeteria's open. I could meet you there in about fifteen minutes."

"Good. I'll be waiting."

She walked briskly to the aisle under the stand.

Brad called Jerry over. "What was that all about?"

Jerry shrugged. "You got me. She comes up and asks me, which one is Brad Stevens."

"That's all?"

"That's it."

Brad walked toward the gym, all sorts of crazy ideas rolling around in his head. *Everybody* was a big slick hash of gossip, personalities, a few name writers, and plenty of bosoms and behinds. What would they want with him? An article? Are quarterbacks naturally over-sexed? Should you do it before a game or does it impair your vitality? He'd never been interviewed by a magazine. This could be the beginning of almost anything.

THE CAFETERIA WAS almost empty as Brad set two cups of coffee on the table.

"It's lousy coffee," he said, sitting down. "The machine never learned how to cook."

She laughed easily. "I'm used to lousy coffee."

Dumping a spray of sugar in his cup, he waited for her to begin.

"You throw a nice football, Brad. Can I call you Brad?"

"Sure."

"That short pitch over the line, I like the way you lead your receiver."

"Hey, a football nut, huh?"

"The worst. A Rams fan, total devotion."

Brad chuckled. "They got a pretty good club this year."

"The best, I hope."

"You do want to talk football, don't you?"

"I always want to talk football, but that's not the angle right now."

He waited, adding a little more sugar.

"Brad, do you remember a girl who used to go to Fort Hanning High, Sally French, who became a model?"

"Sally French?"

"Yes. Tall, beautiful blond hair. . . ."

"Yeah," he said smiling, "I certainly do remember Sally French."

Vida Decker put her purse on the table, took out a small recorder. "Could we talk about Sally?"

"Huh?"

"Let me give you the background. *Everybody* is putting Sally on the front cover of our January issue."

"Sally? Sally French?"

"All by herself."

"Wow," he said softly.

"I'm going to write the copy and captions for the article and pictures. We're bringing our top photographer here for shots of home, girlhood friends, biographical stuff. Then she'll be here for one of the football games, sort of a special homecoming queen, though that might be a bit corny."

"Sally is coming to Fort Hanning?"

"She'll be here next week. She wants to see her folks for a few days, and we can get the background shots."

Brad shook his head slowly. "This is really something, isn't it?"

Vida smiled. She checked the recorder, set it between them. "Will this gadget make you nervous?"

"I don't think so."

"Let's just try." She pressed the "on" button, leaned toward the recorder. "November sixth, Fort Hanning, Bradford Stevens interview." She looked at Brad. "Tell me one of the things you remember best about Sally, Bradford."

Brad grinned at Vida. It was only a test. "Well, I'll tell you one thing, Sally was no great shakes at algebra."

The interview was like old home week. All those things he remembered about Sally, and all those things he remembered but didn't mention about Sally. They came back to him in a warm, wonderful replay of good times. He never thought of the bad times, the down days after he found that Sally's generous nature was not wholly monogamous.

The glow of the interview stayed with him for the rest of the day. Sally was coming back to Fort Hanning. Would he see her? Would she remember him? Well, probably not. Well, why not? Well, look, man, this babe is not a babe anymore. This is a successful cover girl, this is also the girlfriend of Lyle Prescott, star of the silver screen. You will be just a kid quarterback on a hick team, background material for shots of Miss Sally French reliving her carefree girlhood days. So what? You'll see her. And look, man, you've got *memories*.

Brad smiled to himself all that day and woke up Saturday still smiling . . . till he remembered. They were playing Clinton today. The smile was replaced by that familiar tight feeling in the gut at the thought of the opening whistle and the kickoff.

BRAD DRESSED QUIETLY, not wanting to wake his parents. Everyone in the house was tiptoeing, being very polite since the hassle over Alex and the talk about divorce.

On game days, Brad jogged in the morning, had a light lunch, and got to the locker room about one. But today he was early and suited up before most of the players arrived. Was he avoiding Alex, whose locker was next to his? No, he wasn't, he told himself, he just wanted to get ready early, go out and try the turf, see if last night's rain had made it slippery. Bull, Bradford, you're avoiding him, you just can't look him in the eye. Ahh, don't give me that look-in-the-eye crap. He's not looking you in the eye, is he?

By one-thirty the stands were filling. As Brad tossed the ball to the other players warming up, he could glance at the stands, seeing familiar faces. Mr. Prager was there in his usual seat. As Brad ran by he waved, and Mr. Prager waved in return. Of course it was imagination, but Brad thought that Mr. Prager sat very erect and proud, his position seeming to say, I'm Alex's father and I'm glad I'm Alex's father and to hell with the whole lot of you. That's what it seemed like, anyway.

And then, in another part of the stands, there was a fuss as the student ushers found seats for Congressman Van Harper and his party. Brad had received a note that the congressman was lending his presence to the game and would be delighted to see Brad after the expected victory. What a cornball!

From the opening whistle, Clinton gave notice that they were not playing pat-a-cake. A sustained drive with four first downs put them in position for a field goal and they made it. Fort Hanning came back with its own drive and a series of passes that put them on the Clinton thirty. The Fort Hanning stands exploded when Brad scrambled, found a hole in the line, and went through. Alex threw a block at the Clinton safety as Brad went over to score standing up.

Between the halves, a photographer and a reporter from the local paper covered the congressman as had been arranged by the congressman's office. The congressman was photographed with the Fort Hanning cheerleaders, the camera flash capturing Harper's good, clean, Mr. Pure grin. And the reporter quoted his remarks on the value of football as a builder of character.

The game see-sawed wildly with each team having the lead. But in the fourth quarter Brad threw a beautiful bomb to his tight end to give Fort Hanning a seven-point win.

McAveety was riding high with the victory. Two unbeaten years and now only two more games for a third clean season. One of the California state colleges had sent an agent from the athletic department to talk to him. There was a place opening up at Cal State, Fairview, and

McAveety looked like just the man. God was obviously on the job, heading him in the right direction.

Brad hoped to slip out of the locker room quietly but Congressman Harper suddenly boomed in, throwing congratulations right and left, coming down to Brad's locker where the photographer could get a shot of him with his arm around the winning quarterback.

When the hoopla was over, Harper insisted that Brad come down to the Civic Club bar for a quiet drink and a little chat. Brad couldn't figure why they needed a little chat, but Harper was his sponsor for West Point. You don't ignore your sponsor.

CONGRESSMAN HARPER LOUNGED back in the stuffed imitation leather chair at the Civic Club, raised his third bourbon and water to Brad's coke.

"Fort Hanning High, long may it triumph," said Harper.

Brad raised his glass, trying to suppress a terrible urge to yawn. Harper had been going over the game play by play, telling Brad everything that had happened on the field, most of it inaccurate.

"And to a great and future All-American. . . ."

Brad laughed. "Cut it out, Mr. Harper, you're way ahead of me."

"Nonsense." Harper drained his drink, poured himself another. The Civic Club didn't have an actual bar. The members bought their bottles at the adjacent liquor store and mixed their own.

"Nonsense," Harper repeated. "All-American Army quarterback, Bradford Stevens." He smiled. "If, of course, we don't have any problems."

"Problems?" said Brad.

"Yeah." He took a sip of his drink, put it down deliberately.

"Brad . . ."

"Yes, sir."

"Don't 'sir' me, call be Van . . . I'm not that much older'n you are."

"Yes, Van."

"Brad, I think we do have one small problem."

Brad waited.

Harper looked up from his glass. "You'n me. One little problem."

"We have?"

"Yeah. Little now. Could get bigger."

"Like what, Van?"

"Well, mostly an image problem. You follow?"

"Not really."

"Well look . . . take me. Congress of the United States, I've got to project a certain image, right?"

"Well, I guess you do."

"You're damned right I do. We've all got an image we've got to project. To the voters, to the public. Follow?"

Brad shrugged with a half-smile. He was beginning to feel uneasy about the chat.

"Okay . . . I had a good image of you. I put that down on paper, sent it to the Academy with my recommendation." He looked at Brad almost coldly. "I don't want to change that image, Bradford."

"I don't get it."

"Sure you do. You and that Alex what's-his-name. Friends. Best friends. Only, one of you is a homosexual. What does that make the other guy?"

Brad got up slowly from his chair. This was it. Out of nowhere, suddenly, unexpectedly, this was the end of the road to West Point.

"Now I'm not saying anything against you, Bradford, all I'm talking about is that image. What am I going to do about that?"

Brad wanted to throw his coke in Harper's face, punch Mr. Pure to a pulp.

"Mind you, I'm not withdrawing my sponsorship right

this minute. I'm not that kind. I believe in giving the other guy a chance. And that's what I'm giving you, Brad. A chance to change that image. Follow?"

Brad nodded, started toward the door.

"Bradford. . . ."

Harper got up a little unsteadily, went to Brad, held out his hand. "No hard feelings."

"No, sir," said Brad dully.

Harper put his hand on Brad's shoulder. "We're still going to be All-American, they're not going to lick us. Right?"

Brad took a step to the door, opened it.

"I'll be in touch, Bradford. You can call me any time you need me."

Brad walked out of the Civic Club and down Main Street, so angry he felt tears. He hoped to God he wouldn't see anybody he knew.

"No," he'd have to say, "it's just something in my eye, I'm not crying, something blew in out of nowhere, that's all."

Chapter Sixteen

IT WAS THE night of the Music Club concert, when Alex would play his own composition. The music was being taped as his audition for the Music Department at USC. Brad knew how important this evening was for Alex. The athletic scholarship was just about assured, but Alex was determined to make it in the Music Department. Brad picked up his tickets from the dresser and put them in his shirt pocket.

He hadn't really talked to Kay since the incident with Dutch at the Food Factory. But the date for the concert had been set a long while before. He'd take a chance and go by for her and take it from there.

He puttered along listlessly on the bike, not even getting out of low gear. Maybe he didn't want to see Kay, maybe he'd just cool it. Ahh, what the hell, he had the tickets, he might as well use them.

Kay's front door was partly open, which probably meant that he was to go on in. He closed the door, called out to her. "Kay? It's me, I'm here."

Her voice from the bedroom sounded cheerful enough, welcoming. "Be there in a minute. Go downstairs, there's a fantastic new record on the machine."

He didn't want to listen to any fantastic new record, but when Kay said, "Be there in a minute," he knew he was in for a long wait. He checked his watch. They'd probably be late, but Alex's piece wasn't until the second half so maybe it didn't matter.

He went down to the rumpus room, idly scanned the jacket of the new record by a group he'd never heard of.

The picture showed four weird-looking guys with long beards, wearing shorts and riding an elephant. They called themselves "The Indecent Exposure."

Brad plopped down on the sofa. He didn't want to hear a bearded guy in shorts moaning about his baby as he was sure these creeps were bound to do. He rested his head on the back of the sofa. Maybe he ought to take up meditation, something to stop all this useless garbage from sloshing around in his head. What did they do, those meditators? Oh, yeah, they had a word, or a phrase and kept repeating it. There was probably more to it than that, but he guessed that was sort of it. How about "Red sixty-eight, go on two?" He tried that, repeating it over to himself till it didn't have any meaning at all. And then, all of a sudden, there was Kay, standing before him.

"Did I keep you waiting?" she asked breathlessly, having run down the stairs.

Brad shook his head. "No, it's okay."

She turned around, showing her dress. "Like it?"

He thought it was too dressy for the bike, but he said, "Yeah, real nice."

She came over to him, kissed the top of his head. "Don't be so enthusiastic." She sat on the sofa, took his wrist, looked at his watch. "We've got lots of time, haven't we?"

"If you want to miss the first half."

"Why not? It's the full orchestra. I can't stand to see girls blowing tubas, can you?"

What the hell was this? He had almost been expecting her to say she had a date with Dutch or something. And here she was coming on like nothing had happened.

"Don't you want to hear them?" she asked.

"Huh?"

"The Indecent Exposure. They're really out of sight." She bounced up, went to the record player.

"Actually, I don't feel much like hearing them," said Brad.

She stopped with her finger on the "play" button. "What's the matter, Brad?"

"Nothing."

She came back to him. "All right. I was showing off with Dutch. I wanted to hurt you. I guess I did. I'm sorry, Brad, I really am."

"That's okay," he said flatly.

"That's okay? That's all? Just okay?"

"Go ahead, play the record. It can't be as bad as the jacket picture."

She got up again. "Well really, I said I was sorry, isn't that enough?"

"Yeah, that's just fine," Brad said.

She pressed the "play" button with an irritated punch; the record dropped and turned. A heavy booming bass introduced the first weirdo who, sure enough, was wailing for his baby, bawling that she shouldn't have let him down.

Kay returned to the sofa, sitting pointedly at the other end. They listened as all four of the bearded shorts bleated vocally about the baby who had some problems about coming to bed.

I should just move over to her and try to settle it in the usual fashion, Brad thought. She's sorry, isn't that enough? He looked at his watch. The concert had probably already begun.

Kay frowned at him, then scrunched over, took his arm, which was on the back of the sofa, and put it around her shoulder. She leaned her head toward his.

They listened as the four weirdos twanged and boomed and the tenor wailed about the sexual dysfunction of his lady love. Kay pressed closer to Brad, but he decided not to notice.

The record played to the dismal end and stopped. They hadn't spoken or practically moved while The Indecent Exposure blared on.

Brad knew Kay probably intended that they were going

to miss the concert. Alex would come onstage, look for him in the first few rows of seats, and he wouldn't be there. Maybe he could say they came late and had to sit in the last row. Unless he just got up to go right now. Go to the concert.

The arm of the record player came back to the repeat position. The needle touched the spinning disc and the group was back again, wailing for its baby.

Brad listened in numbed silence. Kay kissed him on the ear, but he ignored the invitation. The record ground on.

"Would you like to hear something else?" Kay asked.

"Sure, anything."

She got up, went to the record rack. "Anything special?"

"No, you name it."

Kay picked out a record. "Do we really have to go to the concert?"

"No, I guess not," Brad said.

"I mean, it would be so much nicer just to sit here and listen to our own music, wouldn't it?"

Brad didn't answer.

And that's what they did. Sat and listened to the records. And that was all they did. Just sat there. Hours later, Brad went home. He couldn't remember any time he'd felt lousier, hated himself more. As he was getting undressed he found the tickets in his shirt pocket. He dropped them in the wastebasket and turned out the light. He didn't want to see himself in the mirror.

ALEX SAID "HI" casually the next afternoon as he went past him to the locker. Brad returned the greeting in the same degree. He wanted to say, "I'm sorry I missed your concert, I'm an awful shit and you're better off not knowing me." But he couldn't bring himself to say it.

Alex was suited up first and went out to the field for the practice. That's all they said to each other. Two hi's and that was it. Brad kicked his locker door so hard he could feel his toe stinging.

Dutch Graff looked up from his tied shoelaces and grinned at Brad. "Save your strength, cowboy, you'll need it on the gridiron."

Brad presented Dutch with an obscene gesture involving the middle finger. Dutch laughed and returned it with the slapped arm and raised fist. The other players enjoyed this macho byplay, not knowing what it was all about.

McAveety was easy on them that afternoon. He was riding cloud nine with dreams of leaving Fort Hanning for the post at Cal State. There had been further talk with the agent from the college, with pretty definite commitments on both sides.

When Alex caught a long bomb in the Blue Defense end zone, McAveety actually nodded and said, "Good catch." Everybody on the squad caught Mac's euphoria, and plays ran off like clockwork.

And then, almost on cue, the craziest play of all. Brad had run back to throw a pass. He cocked his arm, pumped a fake toward his wide receiver.

"Brad! Brad Stevens!"

He couldn't help but turn his head toward the sideline and the voice. And there she was in all her cover-girl glory, blond hair shining in the sun. Miss Sally French!

The defense came through and hit Brad with all six hundred pounds of furious young manhood. He went down and out of sight.

"Oh, my God!" Sally cried out, "they've killed him!" She ran onto the field as the players unscrambled and backed off laughing and calling out masculine wow's and hey, mans of approval.

Brad jumped to his feet. Sally flung her arms around him to the cheers of the players.

"Take off that damned bird cage so I can kiss you," said Sally breathlessly.

Brad couldn't believe it. He pulled off his helmet. And

right there in front of twenty-one dirty, sweaty, cheering footballers, Sally French, once the girl of his dreams, now the darling of magazine covers, kissed him.

There was a series of clicks as Eddie Roth, the photographer for *Everybody*, caught the moment. And Vida Decker, grinning broadly on the sideline, was already writing the caption in her head.

McAveety blew his whistle, but the players could tell by his smile that he was going along with it. Eddie Roth got a few quick shots of Mac and that sealed it.

Sally finally let go of Brad. "I'll be staying at my folks' house. I'll call you as soon as I can," she said, and ran off the field to more cheers and calls from the players.

Vida waved to Brad and followed Sally and Eddie Roth off the field. They disappeared under the stands. The whole crazy thing had happened in about two minutes.

McAveety walked over to Brad and smiled as he had when he first discovered Brad's talent. "You got sacked, huh?" he said grinning.

"Yes, sir," said Brad sheepishly.

"Well, that'll learn you to keep your head on the field and off the sidelines."

Brad managed an embarrassed smile.

McAveety looked over the defensive backfield, who themselves were looking toward the stands. "Okay, you horny bastards, we've got a game on Saturday, let's get going!" He blew his whistle for the resumption of play, but he knew their minds weren't going to be entirely on football.

BRAD WALKED OFF the field after practice in a kind of numb, unbelieving daze. It was crazy! She hadn't kissed him right there on the fifty yard line in front of the whole squad! It couldn't have happened! But if you knew Sally, you knew it could. It was like her. But it was just as much like her to have set up the whole thing as a stunt for the magazine.

"Hey, Brad, where were you hiding that one?"

They were starting to ride him. He grinned defensively.

"When do you get to complete that pass, lover boy?"

"Ahh, he'd fumble it."

"Who cares? She can tackle me any day of the week."

Brad had to take it till he was out of the locker room and on the way home. That night he waited in his room for her phone call, but it didn't come. Of course, she'd be terribly busy seeing her folks and all that. He could study while he waited, get going on those miserable French verbs.

He opened to page forty-four. "Conjugation of passive verbs." He read, "The passive verb expresses an action received or suffered by its subject. Example: *Je suis frappé*. I am struck."

He repeated it to himself ten times. *"Je suis frappé."* Well, he was frappéed all right. Two minutes of Sally and the whole world was different. She had that magic, that aura of excitement, that out-of-this-world, one-in-a-hundred quality. Come on, come on Bradford, stick to the verbs. And remember, sonny, you've got other things to worry about. Like what? Well, like Alex, and the congressman for starters. Okay, but how about putting that on the back burner for just a little, I mean, how often do you get kissed by a one-hundred percent, genuine cover girl? Once in a lifetime? So go for it, man! Enjoy. It won't last long, believe me.

Chapter Seventeen

THE SCHOOL WAS in a state of delighted confusion all the next day. They might just as well have closed the place and called it Sally French Day. She had come with the photographer and Vida Decker to invade her old classroom, to pose in the lab with Mr. Matthews, the science teacher, to join the girls' volleyball squad in the gym. Eddie Roth kept clicking away. And everyone wanted to be in the pictures; everyone hoped that come January they'd open *Everybody* magazine and see themselves. Right up there on the printed page with Sally.

In the cafeteria they lined up behind Sally as she pushed her tray along the railing, turning with dazzling smiles as Eddie clicked on shot after shot.

Brad was fascinated by the whole process. He wasn't aware that he was thinking of her as his girl, watching her with hidden pride. He wasn't aware that Kay was watching him watching Sally. He didn't even seem to know that Kay was there at the table right next to him pushing her salad around on her plate, getting more and more irritated.

"I think it's absolutely disgusting," she said.

"Huh?" said Brad.

"The way she peddles sex like it was popsicles or something."

Brad turned to her, amused. "Yeah, that's pretty bad, isn't it?"

"And look at her, look at those phony jeans she's wearing."

"Yeah," said Brad appreciatively.

"I'd hate to see her try to sit down in those things."

"Me, too," Brad said.

"She probably had them 'specially made at two hundred dollars a pair."

"And they don't even fit," he said grinning.

"Very funny," said Kay getting up from her chair.

"Hey, where're you going?"

"I'm going out to the front lawn and upchuck my lunch, that's where I'm going." And that's where she went. Though whether she actually upchucked her lunch, Brad had no way of knowing. His eyes returned to Sally, who had now come to the end of the line and was allowing Eddie to pay for the lunch. Brad saw her say something to Eddie, then pick up her tray and head in his direction.

Ohmygod, he thought, she isn't going to sit with me!

But she most certainly was. He jumped up and took her tray.

"Man," she said, blowing hair out from in front of her face. "I am licked, pooped, dead on my feet."

Brad set down her tray, chuckling as he looked at her.

"What's the matter?" she asked.

"Nothing," he said. "I just wanted to see if you could sit down in those pants."

She sat down, entirely without trouble. He continued to look at her, not noticing that everyone in the entire cafeteria was looking at them. He sat down slowly, moved closer to her.

She smiled at him, put her hand over his. "Later, Brad," she said wearily. "Just you and me. Later."

HE FLOATED THROUGH his two after-lunch classes, unaware that he had conjugated his passive verbs correctly and had given a quite credible five-minute overview of Hamlet's problems with his mother.

At the end of classes he waited, hoping to see her before football practice, but she was in the auditorium doing

something with the school choir. He remembered that she
was very big in the choir back in her school days.

He went through practice in a warm fog, letting himself
get caught in the pocket twice. He didn't notice that the
other players, thinking back to yesterday, were especially
easy on him. All except Dutch, who tried to set up a blitz
with the idea of crippling him, but Alex read the move
and blocked it. He thanked Alex and got a quiet, "That's
okay." And, Brad wondered, did he do it for me, or was
it because he's a smart footballer? He was relieved when
practice was over.

The school seemed almost empty when he came out
from the gym, with no sign of Sally French and Company.
He figured she'd gone home. Oh well, "later" meant later,
didn't it?

He got on his bike and putted slowly out of the parking
lot. Then he saw her. She was coming down the steps of
the main building. Eddie Roth was crouching down, getting an angle. Brad wasn't close enough to see that she
was so worn out she could hardly smile. She stopped at
Eddie's command and summoned one last dazzler. Then
she saw Brad, burst into tears, and ran toward him.

He turned, wheeled toward her, stopped. She threw one
leg over the seat, grabbed him around the waist. "Get out
of here!" she cried. "Go on before he catches us!"

She leaned her head against his shoulder as the bike
zoomed off and out on the road.

"Where to?" Brad asked.

"Anywhere," she said. "Just go."

He gave it the gun and headed out of town. With her
cheek pressed against his back and the tears wetting his
shirt, Sally held on tightly. Brad could feel her arms
around him. "Later," she had said. "Just you and me,
later."

SHE DIDN'T SAY a word for a long time and when they got
out to the state road that led up into the mountains he

asked if she wanted to go back. He could feel her head against his shoulders shaking a no.

The day was still warm, with the red tint of late afternoon making a deeper green in the fields, bolder shadows on the tall trees that lined the highway. Brad lazed along, feeling the wonderful closeness of Sally. He didn't dare ask himself how all of this had happened; he just gave in to the moment, decided to let it ride.

After a while he could feel Sally sit up straighter. He turned his head, smiled at her. She tightened her arms around him. A truck passed and blasted its horn, whether in joy at the sight of them or in anger they couldn't tell, but soon Brad turned off the highway and onto a narrow blacktop.

The road wound into the hills past small farms with pickups in the yard and children chasing chickens. Sally waved to a tall skinny boy shooting baskets against a garage door. The boy waved back and leaped to dunk the ball, as though just for her.

"Brad. . . ."

"Yeah?"

"We've been here before."

He grinned. "I was wondering if you would remember."

"Green something. Green Lake?"

"Pond. Green Pond. Okay?"

She laughed. "It's the only place in the world I want to be right this minute."

He gunned the bike a little and in minutes they were at the gates of the small state park and picnic ground. At the end of the summer the gates were closed, and now the tables around the pond that gave the place its name were deserted.

They climbed the fence. Brad took her hand, leading her on a wooded trail that wound around the edge of the pond.

She leaned her head against his shoulder as they walked.

"Brad . . . why did I think of you and not anybody else?"

"Huh?"

"When they asked me to do the piece. For *Everybody*. Vida talked to me for hours getting the story. And there you were on almost every page."

Two years later and he couldn't help feel a jealous stab.

"What about Mickey Dover, and Red Elton, and Charley Case. Where were they?"

She laughed. "Oh, Mickey Dover, whatever happened to Mickey?"

"I haven't got the foggiest idea," Brad said sharply.

"And Red Elton. All those crazy kids. . . ."

"Crazy kids?"

"Oh, Brad, they didn't mean anything. . . ."

"I know. Nothing meant anything. You were so wrapped up in yourself."

She stopped, looked up at him soberly. "I sure was." She shook her head. "I must've been an awful pain in the ass."

"You were."

"But you loved me."

"I sure did."

"And I loved you."

"Sally. . . ."

"Yes?"

"Bullshit."

She smiled tenderly, put her arms around him. They kissed, a long remembering kiss. She moved back, took his hand, and they continued on the path.

Oh God, Brad thought, she's so wonderful I could forgive anything. Now come on, Bradford, cut the kid stuff, this is Sally French, cover girl, and she's all alone with you in these beautiful woods and you're talking about forgiving her? Man, you are one helluva way off base, believe me. You ought to be glad she even looks at you.

Which she did at that moment. So they stopped and kissed again, this time longer, holding each other close, and finally he was the one who broke away. Because, like all damned fool males, he had to ask that question.

"What about Mr. Movie Star? Lyle Prescott?"

"What?"

"I saw your picture with him in this magazine."

"Lyle?" She laughed. "Oh, Bradford, really."

"What do you mean, 'Oh, Bradford really'?"

"He's fifty-*two*, Brad. And alcoholic, and no good to any female for years now. Everybody knows that."

"Oh, they do?"

"But he's a darling. A wonderful, kind, sweet darling. I try to keep him sober and prop him up at parties. He likes to be seen with me and I need to be seen with him. It's an arrangement."

"I guess I shouldn't have asked. It's none of my business."

"It certainly isn't. But you had to ask. Or else how could you still love me?"

They stopped walking again and this time they sank to their knees and lay in the soft grass at the edge of the pond. And even though he didn't wholly believe her about Mickey and Red and Charley—and even about that ancient star of the silver screen—she seemed all the fabulous things he had ever dreamed about her. Oh, Sally!

WHEN THE SUN was nearly gone and cold air was slipping down the mountain, Sally suddenly sat up. She had fallen asleep as Brad had watched her, her damp hair resting on his arm that was buried in the grass. Now, Sally leaned over and smoothed his rumpled hair, touched the strong curve of his neck. He rolled over, smiled up at her.

"I guess we'd better go," he said.

She leaned down, kissed him. He put his arms around

her, drew her to him. They lay there, close together for a moment. And he smiled and said again, "I really think we'd better go."

IT WAS ALMOST dark when they got up and looked around at the last glow of light reflecting off the pond. She took his hand and they walked slowly back to the bike. He helped her over the fence, though she didn't need help. On the other side they just stood there clinging to each other, not wanting it to end.

Winding down the blacktop road with the single headlight creating a dome of shadow in the trees overhead, Sally held tightly to Brad's back. It was getting cold, but they didn't really feel it. Their close-pressed bodies almost seemed to speak for them, saying, this is okay, this can go on forever.

But it went on just as far as Sally's house.

"Will I see you before you go?" he asked.

"Saturday. I'll be at the trophy dinner."

"Not before?"

"I can't tomorrow. Vida's got me all day, family stuff."

The porch light went on; they moved away from each other.

" 'Night," she said softly, and ran to the front door.

He watched till the door shut him off, then he got back on the bike and went home.

His mother had left a cold supper for him on the kitchen table. She played bridge on Thursday nights and he had the kitchen to himself. He liked to read at supper, but tonight even the sports page couldn't get his attention. He read that Army was ready for Notre Dame but it didn't sink in, even though he was intensely interested in Deel, the Army quarterback, wondering, hoping, dreaming of himself as maybe being in that position someday.

He heard his father's car go through the porte cochere. His father had been staying late at the post, claiming heavy work, but Brad sensed that they were avoiding each other, his father and mother.

The outside door opened. His father came in with Mug, who ran to Brad with tail wagging.

"Hi, Dad."

"Evening, Bradford."

Brad nodded to the plate of cold meat and salad. "Mom left supper."

"Thanks. I ate at the post."

His father stood there awkwardly, not able to find a pleasantry to end the brief exchange. He held up his leather case. "I'll be in my study if you need me."

"Okay, Dad."

His father left the kitchen to go up the back stairs to his study. What a weird thing to say. "If you need me." He rubbed the silky fur on Mug's neck. If I really needed him, he wouldn't be there. He'd say, "you're big enough to do that or decide that on your own." Brad thought of Alex's father. Of Mr. Prager that night, putting his arms around Alex, loving him.

Mug whined when Brad stopped the neck rub. Suddenly Brad didn't feel hungry. Piece by piece he took the cold meat off his plate and tossed it to Mug.

Then he pushed his chair back from the table and said the magic word. "Run?" Mug whined and danced, skidding on the kitchen floor. Brad opened the back door to let him out.

Running. Maybe that was the way to solve everything, just keep running. Or, thought Brad as he moved down the empty street, was running away from everything really possible?

Chapter Eighteen

HE TRIED TO avoid Ellie when they came out of the biology lecture, but the press of students in the hall pushed them closer. It wasn't that he didn't like her. He thought very highly of Ellie, but he knew they'd have to talk about one of the things he didn't even want to think about that particular morning.

"Hi," Ellie said shyly.

"Hi," Brad said with a forced smile. "Where you been all this time?"

"Around. Keeping busy."

"Show biz, huh?" He was forcing the casualness.

"What?" Ellie said.

"Drama Club."

"Oh yes, lots of Drama Club."

They walked a few steps in silence. He knew he'd have to ask about the concert. He hadn't run into anyone he knew who'd been there. Of course, he'd seen Alex yesterday, but he'd been too embarrassed to ask him about it. "How was it, Ellie? The concert. Alex's composition."

She didn't answer immediately.

"I missed it," he said. "I was going to go but . . ."

"He played beautifully. They loved it."

He blew a relieved breath. "I'm glad."

"Most of them loved it." She stopped, turned to him, forcing him to stop and look at her. "Dutch Graff and three of the football players were there and they left the auditorium when Alex came onstage."

"Oh, no."

"Everybody turned to look. I guess they all knew what it meant. Then someone started to applaud for Alex."

"It must've been you."

"I don't know. But there were some of us. He didn't seem to notice. He just sat down and played. At the end the noise was like a bomb going off. They stood up and clapped and clapped as if they'd never stop." Ellie held back the tears, but they were in her voice as she told it.

Brad didn't have anything to say.

Luckily Sarah Graves, Ellie's friend, came up behind them just then and took Ellie's arm. "Hi," Sarah said. "I missed half the lecture. Did you take notes, Ellie? 'Lo, Brad."

"Hi, Sarah."

"Yes, I took notes," Ellie said. Then, to him: "We'll see you later, Brad."

He watched as the girls went down the hall, arm in arm, to an empty room where Sarah could copy the notes. Brad walked slowly out the door. There was a bench under a big sycamore tree in the side yard. He sat on the bench a long time, trying to hold the guilty feeling at a distance, trying to define what he really felt, kicking it around so much that he didn't know how anything felt. His head was resting in his hands, his elbows on his knees, as if this classic position could help his inner struggle.

He became aware of someone sitting beside him.

"Alex didn't say anything about your not being there," said Ellie. "But I think he understood."

Brad sat up. "Sure he understood," he said angrily. "I might just as well have walked out of the hall with Dutch Graff."

"No, I don't think he felt that."

"Why not! I could put up a sign on the scoreboard. I'm dropping my friend Alex because he's gay and I don't want anybody to think I am, too! Three-foot-high letters!"

Ellie touched his hand, which was gripping the bench. "Yes, that's the way it looks. But I know it isn't so."

"Ellie, Ellie, grow up, will you?"

She smiled tenderly. "I know it isn't so, Brad."

THE GAME WITH Monroe High was a breeze. Monroe was one for six on the season and no match for the powerful Fort Hanning offense. In the second half, Mc-Aveety sent in all the promising rookies, leaving only his veteran backfield. The score piled up and on the last bomb the Monroe safety hit Alex from behind a split second too soon. Alex went down with his knee beneath him. He had to be helped off the field as the stands watched in silence.

Monroe got the maximum penalty on the play, but it didn't matter. The final score was Fort Hanning forty-seven, Monroe nothing.

EVERY YEAR THE game before the last was Trophy Night, sponsored by the senior class. The gym was turned over to a class committee, which arranged the music and decorations. A stage was set up at one end of the gym for the music and awarding of trophies. Around the stage were tables where refreshments were served for the seniors and their dates. The athletic department had a special table, and tonight its own celebrity, Miss Sally French, herself not too far removed in time from her own graduation night two years ago.

In order to save money the dance committee decided to go disco. With lots of flashing lights and Stubby Johnson's eighty-watt speakers, they could play records and have enough money for sandwiches and an elegant punch. And if someone had slipped a quantity of vodka into the punch, certainly no one could blame the committee.

Brad's date with Kay for Trophy Night was something long understood, but he'd called her to confirm it. Brad got the car for the night and arrived for her promptly at eight. Since the night they had missed Alex's concert, they hadn't spoken on the phone or even met at the usual table in the cafeteria. Surprisingly, Kay was ready promptly.

She did look lovely, he thought, in the deep red party dress that Norma, her father's girl friend, had insisted she borrow for the occasion. Norma, just a few years older than Kay, would probably be her step-mother in the near future and since they were the same size, why not?

Brad gave an appreciative wow when she appeared at the door. The wow was followed by a big flash of guilt. Usually he'd take her in his arms or give her a kiss in appreciation. But she cut it short with: "Hi, am I late?" and walked quickly ahead of him to the car.

They didn't talk much in the two miles to the school. When they parked, he tried to ease it a little. "We're sitting with Chuck and Alice. That okay with you?"

"It doesn't really matter," said Kay.

He locked the car and offered her his arm.

"I could get us a table alone, if you'd rather."

She stopped, looked at him coolly. "Are you making conversation?"

"Yeah, I guess I am."

"Well, you don't have to."

He couldn't help it. He said: "Maybe you'd rather sit with Dutch Graff. I could fix that."

He could see that was too much. She was on the edge of tears. "I'm sorry, I didn't mean that."

"I'd rather not go to this party at all," she said, "but I haven't got the nerve to back out with everybody watching. So let's go."

It was going to be a long evening, he could tell that.

The blast of sound was almost solid as they opened the gym door. The red and amber revolving lights whirled around the dancers and bounced off the silver trophies exhibited on the award stand.

They made their way through the dancers to the senior tables. Chuck waved to them and Kay went ahead quickly. Then Brad saw Sally, seated at the athletes' table with Coach McAveety. His heart pounded as if he were doing sprints when he passed and saw her lips form, ever so slightly, a not-so-hidden kiss.

He sat down at their own table and gratefully sipped the already spiked punch that Chuck shoved his way. It was impossible to talk above the sound of the music, so they drank the punch and after it had eased the way, they danced.

An hour later it was time to award the trophies. Everyone believed that Brad would get Most Valuable Player, but there was much speculation on the lesser awards. Just like giving the Oscars on TV, the awards committee strung out the minor distinctions: Player Who Improved the Most, Best Defensive Back, stuff like that.

Each award was greeted with cheers and a roll of drums. Stubby Johnson had borrowed a sound-effects record and spotted it carefully to produce the illusion. Up on the stage, McAveety was riding high. A beautiful girl at his side, the warming punch in his middle, and him the master of ceremonies giving away the prizes to the poor, overworked players he'd been hassling all season. Go, McAveety!

Then came the hitch. McAveety picked up the envelope, read it aloud. "Most Completed Passes This Season." He frowned. He should have asked the committee what was coming. In the silence that followed he opened the envelope, repeated the citation. "Most Completed Passes This Season . . . Alex Prager."

Stubby rolled the electronic drums, there was scattered applause. But very scattered.

McAveety looked around the senior tables. "Is Alex Prager here?" He knew Alex was at home in bed with his twisted knee.

Brad had not expected this any more than McAveety. He knew damned well he ought to stand up right now and say he'd accept the award for his friend, Alex. Do it,

Brad. Go do it now. Hurry, this is your chance to show Alex how you feel. Accept the award, accept Alex!

McAveety put the trophy back on the stand, picked up another envelope. "I guess someone will get that to Prager," he mumbled, and quickly read off the name of the next winner.

Brad sat through the rest of the awards kicking himself around, and when it came his turn to stand up and be told that he was The Most Valuable Player, it was just a great big anticlimax. He managed to smile through the cheers and applause of his teammates and friends, but he got back to his seat in a hurry, glad that the whole thing was over at last.

Chapter Nineteen

THE PUNCH BOWL came back from a mysterious journey to the kitchen, and the dancing took on a wild new turn. Brad was hardly in the mood for it. He scarcely noticed when Dutch came over and took Kay out on the floor. He didn't even notice Sally, who was almost surrounded by the football team, each of whom fancied she was dancing with him alone.

Brad got up and took his glass of punch to the side door. He opened it and went outside. The silence was like a cool towel after a long hot run. He sat on a stone bench looking up at the stars and the thin crescent of the moon.

He sat for a long time running it over in his head. This should be the big night of the year. Most Valuable Player, an unbeaten season, next fall West Point, a limitless future, everything going for him. Man, you've got it made. Stop dragging ass, go in there and dance your head off, this year will never come around again.

He drank the rest of the punch, crumpled the plastic cup. He sat very still. Some time later he heard the gym door open, the music blasted out, then again the wonderful silence. He turned idly. It was Sally.

He jumped up as she came over to him.

"Let's walk," she said.

He took her hand. "Where?"

"Anywhere."

They walked, hand in hand, down the path toward the football field. There was a cinder track in front of the stands. They walked minutes in silence around the field where only hours before Brad had thrown the pass to Alex.

Finally they stopped and she reached up and kissed him. Brad nodded toward the first row of seats. He took off his coat and put it around her shoulders. They sat close together with his arm around her.

"Sally?" he said.

"Mm?"

"I've been thinking about this for a long while." He didn't realize he was lying, but he was. He'd been thinking about it for the past two minutes, but it seemed so absolutely right, so perfect, that he must have been thinking about it all day. Or the last two years, for that matter.

"About what?" Sally asked.

"Us."

She laughed. "Us?"

"You and me."

"Something profound, huh? Very heavy."

"Believe me, it is," he said.

"Like I'm going tomorrow and you'll miss me."

"Worse."

"I'll miss you," she said.

"Will you, Sally?"

"What do you think?"

"I think" . . . he took a deep breath. "I think . . . now listen, Sally, I'm serious, this isn't too much punch talking . . ."

"Kiss me instead."

He kissed her. A long kiss.

"Again," she said.

"No, you've got to listen. Sally, I've had an offer from a pro team, to go to their farm, the money's really good . . ."

"Brad. . . ."

"Now, listen, I could take care of you. I mean, it's not big money, the kind I'll make later. . . ."

"Darling, darling. . . ." she put her fingers to his lips. "Come off the cloud."

"But I mean it, Sally."

She kissed his ear. "I know you do. It's wonderful, I love it, I've never heard anything so beautiful. Now let's say good-bye just the way we knew we'd have to. Big, grown-ups. . . ."

"You're putting me down."

"No, no." She dropped the coat and put her arms around him. "Never. I'd never put you down." She held him close. "You're too dear to me. But don't you see . . ."

"Sure, I see. The cover girl and the high school kid." He shook his head, moved back from her. "Yeah, I knew it wouldn't work. But it's like that long bomb when you're trailing and the clock's running out. You've got to try."

"I'd hate it if you didn't." She looked around the field. "Are we going to say good-bye right here on this hard bench?"

"You wanted to be grown-up."

"Not that grown-up," she said. "Did they ever put a new lock on the supply shed?"

"No, they never did."

They joined hands and started off the field toward the supply shed on the other side of the gym. But they never made it. As they passed the gym, the door opened and Vida Decker came walking out.

"Well, there you are," she said to Sally. She pointed to her watch. "Eleven-thirty. We're ready to roll. Eddie's got the car out in front."

"Two minutes," said Sally.

"Okay," said Vida. She waved. "So long, Brad. Thanks for helping."

"Good-bye, Vida."

Vida closed the door.

Sally put her arms around him. "It'll always be you," she said softly. "No matter what." She kissed him fleetingly and ran to the gym door. She stopped a moment as the wild music blasted out. That was the picture of her he would always remember. Standing in the doorway of the gym, blowing a last kiss. *So long, Sally.*

He stood there for a long time, then turned and walked slowly back to the field. He stopped once, looked toward the gym. He ought to go back to the party. Kay would wonder what had happened to him, and she'd be right.

What if he told her what did happen? What if he leveled with her, said, look, Sally French has been inside my head all these years and I didn't know it. Oh, bull, Bradford, that is a lot of crap, and you know that, too. Kay's a terrific girl and she's the one who's been in your head, and Sally comes in out of the blue, and all of a sudden you're practically asking her to marry you.

So what? So I meant it. Every word. I'd go right back and say it all over again. Sure you would, screwball, because you don't know where you're at. You've got the value judgments of a tomcat. What the hell would Grandpa Stevens say if you laid this mess on him?

Brad found himself back at the stands. He sat down, swung his feet up on the bench. After a moment he lay back, clasped his hands under his head, and looked up at the stars, searching for his favorite constellations, putting off thinking. There's Orion, there's Taurus, and there's Andromeda, his favorite of the November night. He closed his eyes.

He woke suddenly, sat up. He could hear the sound of the cars leaving the parking lot. He looked at his watch. *Ohmygod,* the party's over!

He hurried back to the gym. Stubby was still shaking the walls with his music, but there were only a few couples on the floor. The table where he'd been sitting was empty. He caught Chuck and Alice as they were crossing the floor to go.

"Where's Kay?" he asked Chuck.

Alice answered instead with an undertone of malice.

"She left more than an hour ago. She said she could find someone to take her home."

"Thanks," said Brad as Chuck and Alice made their way to the door.

He stood there a moment. The music stopped and Stubby put on another disc. It was the good night song telling everyone that it was all over.

Brad went toward the table where his trophy stood in a mess of refreshments. He passed the trophy stand, stopped. Alex's trophy was still there. He looked at it for a long time, then he picked it up and went to his table.

The parking lot was almost empty. He walked toward his car dangling the two trophies at his side the way he'd dragged his helmet after a rough time on the field—beat, drained, feeling washed up. And on Trophy Night, that big night of the year. What a bummer.

He opened the car door, set the trophies on the seat, put the key in the ignition. Maybe he ought to go to Kay's house right now, straighten it out, tell her he was sorry.

For what? For everything. For the way they'd been moving apart these last few weeks. Talk it out, level with each other. What's *she* got to level about? It's you, stupid, you're the one who got it all screwed up in the first place.

He turned the key, backed out of the parking space. Okay, that's what he'd do. Right now. So it's two A.M. Her father's away. Maybe she'd even be waiting for him. Well sure, that's it, she could be waiting for him. Sure, she's probably been crying a little, but he'd take her in his arms, comfort her, tell her everything's all right now.

He drove a little faster as he pictured the scene, his apology, her forgiving kiss, the sofa in the rumpus room. Hurry up, Brad, she's waiting.

He drove too fast but got to Kay's house safely. The front door was locked. He rang the bell impatiently. No answer. He rang again. He ran around to the kitchen door, looked through the window. She was sitting at the kitchen table, coffee cup in front of her.

He knocked on the door. She didn't even turn. He pushed on the door. It was open. He went in quickly, put his hands on her shoulders, and kissed the top of her head.

"Kay, I'm sorry."

She didn't move.

He came around in front of her, sat down beside her, took her hand. "Kay . . . I'm sorry."

"For what?" she said dully.

"For everything. Whatever it is. I'm sorry, I really am."

She looked at him for the first time. He could see that she had been crying. "I am too, Brad," she said.

He smiled tenderly. "No, not you. Me."

"No, me. I'm sorry about you and me. That I ever loved you as much as I did, that I ever let you be my whole life."

"Kay, listen, baby . . ."

"No, you listen. My whole life. Morning, noon, and night, that's all I think of, just you. Did you know that?"

"Sure, and I think of you."

"Oh, stop it, Brad. Where have you been these last few days? With her, picking up where you left off two years ago before you bounced off her and found me."

"Kay, listen to me. Let's go back to square one."

"That's right, you found me, a nothing, and you felt sorry for me."

"What's that got to do with now?" he asked. "Nothing's changed with you and me."

"Nothing's changed! Where have you been hiding! Am I number one anymore? Do you ever think of me when we're not making out! You put me down in front of everyone, leave me sitting at the table. People come up, where's Brad, have you seen Brad? Oh yes, I've seen him, he just sneaked out, over there by the side door. And *she* went out after him. No, I don't know what they're doing, but I can guess. Brad, how can you drag me down like that!"

"Kay, I never intended . . ."

"Where do I stand with you? Number three, number four? Who's on first? Sally French? Your precious Alex?"

"Let's not go into Alex."

"Why not? He's really number one, isn't he? Hasn't he always been? Isn't your first concern Alex? You don't need me, Brad, you've got a girl friend and a boy friend all in one."

He slammed his fist on the table. "Goddammit, Kay, you've got no right to say that!"

She got up from the table. "I'm going to bed, Brad. You might as well go home. I don't want to see you anymore."

"That's all right with me," he said angrily.

She walked to the doorway of the kitchen. He ran suddenly, put his arms around her. She didn't move. Her eyes filled with tears.

"No, Brad, that won't work."

He held her, turned her head, kissed her. She made no response. He let her go.

"Please don't call me. I don't want to talk to you."

"I'll call you in the morning," he said.

"I won't answer."

She walked down the hall into her bedroom and closed the door.

He knew she meant it.

Chapter Twenty

HE HEARD THE rain thumping on the roof. He might as
well go back to sleep. What time was it? He opened one
eye not wanting to wake himself completely. Eight-thirty.
Gloomy Sunday. He closed the eye, drifted on the alpha
wave, rocking gently toward sleep. Then bang, reality. He
sat up. The fight with Kay. "I don't want to see you anymore." Sally gone. "It'll always be you." Alex's trophy. "I
guess someone will get that to Prager." Leftover dialogue
from Trophy Night hit like the pounding rain.

He dressed reluctantly, not wanting to get involved in
Sunday. He sat down at his desk to put on his sneakers.
Well, there it was, the trophy. "Most Completed Passes
This Season . . . Alex Prager." He'd have to take it to
Alex.

Now wait a minute, chum, what's this "have to"
business? *Want to,* that's what you mean. Alex deserves
it. The trophy will make him feel good, help that
knee. And listen, it won't hurt his prospects for USC, either. They'll go a long way to get a better receiver than
Alex Prager. Matter of fact, they'll be damned lucky to
get him at all. Not only ball catcher, but piano player and
math whiz. And by God, one helluva fine all-around guy.
They'd be damned lucky to get him.

Brad rummaged the closet for his windbreaker, the one
with the hood for rainy days. He'd have breakfast with
Alex, cheer him up. With that knee, Alex wouldn't start
in the final game next Saturday. Do something to make
him feel better. Hey, how about bringing breakfast in a
backpack as a gag. Alex would remember what it meant.

145

It would remind him of that marvelous stunt Alex pulled the last time Brad was sick in bed.

When was that? Last summer? Summer before? Maybe even before that. Oh, that was a crazy night all right. Let's see. Brad was sixteen? Fifteen going on sixteen? Well, the hell with when it was.

They had planned a trip to Chinese Camp along the old gold trail. Two days before, Brad phoned Alex.

"I can't go," Brad had said.

"You can't go?"

"No, I can't go. I'm in bed."

"You're in bed?"

"Yeah, I'm in bed."

"How come you're in bed at seven o'clock at night?"

"Because I've got the lousy chicken pox!"

"Chicken pox!" And Alex began to laugh.

"Don't laugh, you jerk, I look like a case of leprosy. And you can't come near me, and I've got to stay in bed in my room for the rest of the week!"

But Alex didn't hear that, he just couldn't stop laughing.

So Brad stayed in bed and even though Alex came to the house, Brad's mother wouldn't let him in. Brad was contagious, she said.

The night before they were supposed to go to Chinese Camp it was eleven o'clock and everybody in Fort Hanning was in bed, including Brad's father and mother. But Brad was awake, reading, itching, slightly feverish, mad at the whole world.

Then he heard this kind of creaky noise just under his window. Brad's bedroom was on the top floor of the old mansion. It had a bay window shaded by a magnificent fig tree that towered forty feet from the ground and thrust a large limb over the roof of the second floor just below his window.

And on that limb, thirty feet above the ground, with a

full pack on his back, was Alex, inching his way toward the roof.

Brad swung the casement out as Alex touched his foot on the roof of the second floor. He grabbed Brad's outstretched hand. Brad hauled him up and through the window.

Brad was laughing and puffing. "You idiot, what's the idea?"

Alex shook off the pack. "The idea is, you can't go camping, camping comes to you."

"Oh, man, you are the screwiest!"

"Yeah," said Alex, opening the pack, taking out the food. "Steak, canned beans, bread."

Brad grabbed it. "Kaluha!"

"You can't drink, you're sick."

"I just got well."

They both laughed and unloaded the stuff. Brad got out his Coleman stove to cook the steak. And how they got away with all this, he could never remember. They ate steak and drank the Kaluha, and everything they said seemed funny.

"I mean, man, you know what you looked like crawling along that branch?" Brad said, chewing steak. "You looked like that creepy guy in that horror movie, that what's-his-name."

"The hunchback guy."

"Yeah, Quasimodo of Notre Dame, that's what you looked like."

They laughed and Alex said, "Hey, listen, if we make the team this year, that's what I could be, left hunchback."

That broke them up, the left hunchback of Fort Hanning High. But they had to shut up quick when a door opened downstairs. Luckily it closed again. Yeah, everything they said sounded funny and they drank and ate till one A.M. It was the greatest camping ever.

Alex was in no condition to climb down the tree, so

they snuck him down the back stairs. When he fell the last six steps and fled into the night, it was a very touchy moment. But Kitty found only Brad in the kitchen getting a glass of milk. She looked at his flushed face and sent him back to bed.

Two weeks later, Alex got the chicken pox.

BRAD LIKED WALKING in the rain. He had the trophy in his pack and an outdoors-type breakfast for both himself and Alex. He didn't know what he was going to say to Alex. Maybe just hand him the trophy and let it happen from there. Yeah, that was the best. Just bringing the thing would say plenty.

He walked faster, enjoying the stinging raindrops, licking them off his lips, sure that no one was watching this early on Sunday morning.

When he got to the Prager house, he saw the open garage door and Mr. Prager working on the engine of his car. Mr. Prager straightened up when he saw Brad. He smiled, beckoned Brad to come over.

"Bradford, what are you doing out in the rain?"

Brad felt good in the welcoming warmth of that smile. "Coming to see one of the Bums working on Sunday as usual."

Mr. Prager laughed. "Caught me, didn't you?"

"Yes, sir." Brad gestured toward the house. "How's Alex?"

"Okay, considering," said Mr. Prager. "He can stand all right, but he can't walk much."

"Has he had breakfast yet?"

"I dunno, Brad, I've been out here since six."

Brad unshouldered the pack. "I brought something for him and me, kind of a camping gag. I though we could eat it together."

Mr. Prager frowned slightly. "Oh, breakfast, huh?"

"Yeah, it's an old thing we had, you probably don't remember . . ."

"Brad . . ." Mr. Prager interrupted, something he didn't do very often.

"Yes, sir."

Mr. Prager hesitated a moment. "Listen, son . . . I know you well enough, I mean, you and me, we don't have to beat around the bush, do we?"

"No sir, we don't," said Brad.

"Well, I'll lay it on the line, Bradford. Alex doesn't want to see you. He told me in case you might be coming over."

The shock of it didn't show on Brad's face.

"I mean, I don't know what's going on with you two . . ." Mr. Prager stopped. "Well, yes, yes, I do know what's going on. I mean . . ." It was hard for him to say it. "I mean, there's Alex's problem."

Brad touched Mr. Prager on the shoulder. "Look, I'm sorry, I should've known better."

"No, no, I shouldn't have said it so plain out, he doesn't want to see you. What I mean . . ."

"It's okay, Mr. Prager."

"Brad, listen, if it was me . . ."

"I know, that's okay."

"It isn't, Brad. You two guys were the greatest together. I mean, you knew all about him and even so . . ."

"We'll work it out, Mr. Prager." He opened the flap of the pack. "There's something I brought for Alex. You can give it to him. He won it last night."

He handed the trophy to Mr. Prager.

"For Alex?"

"Read what it says."

Mr. Prager read the inscription slowly. "Most Completed Passes . . ."

"He's the best, Mr. Prager."

Mr. Prager held the trophy tenderly, reading again. "He was the best, wasn't he? That first touchdown you threw him yesterday . . ."

"Nobody could catch that one but Alex. It was fantastic."

"Yeah, it was, wasn't it." Mr. Prager kept looking at the trophy, his head down, not wanting Brad to see his feelings. "Thanks, Brad."

"That's okay," said Brad, picking up his pack. He put his arms through the loops. "I'll be seeing you, Mr. Prager."

"Yeah, sure, any time," said Mr. Prager. "Be glad to see you."

Brad stepped into the rain. He wanted to get away fast so Mr. Prager wouldn't call him back. Or maybe he wouldn't go quite that fast, in case Mr. Prager did call him back. Ahh, the hell with it. If Alex didn't want to see him, okay, he didn't want to see Alex. I mean, there I am making this move and he's cutting me off. Okay, Alex, two can play cut-off, if that's what you want.

The rain didn't feel that good on his face now. He blew it away in angry puffs. Yes, sir, two can play. Hey, wait a minute. Supposing it was that old thing with Alex. I mean, supposing he's pulling that I'm-poison-keep-away bit, protecting me again. He could do it, the crazy jerk, he could be turning me off for my own good, he's dumb enough. Well no, not dumb, stubborn. If he thought he was helping me he would, the nutty bastard. Or would he?

Suddenly, the wind rose, whipped the rain into Brad's face, stung his cheeks. He hunched his shoulders, pulled the hood of his jacket over his forehead.

And looking down from his bedroom, the rain sheeting against the window, Alex saw his friend Brad leaning head-down into the wind. There was something so vulnerable about the bent back, the bowed head barely visible under the hood.

Robin was right, Alex thought. I can never tell Brad how I really feel about him . . . and I never will. He sighed, pressed his forehead against the rain-spattered window. *So long, Brad. So long, pal.*

Through the streaming window, Alex watched Brad skirt a puddle, then turn the corner. *Go, Brad, go.*

BRAD TURNED DOWN his street. What he needed was someone to talk to. Then it hit him with a sinking blow. Kay wasn't going to be around anymore. He'd been keeping that one in the back of his mind, but it jabbed him hard.

No Kay. No arm around his shoulder telling him he was the greatest thing that ever came down the highway, no loving moments, problem-solving with bodies close, arms around each other. Man, you're blowing everything, right and left, aren't you?

Mug was waiting on the porch. When he saw Brad, he bounded down the steps. Brad stopped under the porte cochere, knelt down, and roughed Mug's head in Mug's favorite way. The mutt growled happily, biting at Brad's sleeve. Brad stood up. "Run?" Mug danced with joy.

Brad dropped the pack on the porch steps. With Mug bouncing ahead, he jogged down the wet street. One thing about dogs, they don't ask questions, they don't doubt you, they don't demand anything. A lot to be said for dogs. People could learn plenty if they really paid attention.

Chapter Twenty-one

PRACTICE THAT WEEK was very serious, the last game of
the season coming up, Fort Hanning undefeated. The
emotional load was on Fort Hanning, not Jefferson High.
Jefferson had nothing to lose. They were five for two;
they could retrieve their season by dumping the undefeated.

McAveety was just as tense as his players, but he
couldn't show it. His job was to keep them on edge without overworking them. If he won this one he could see
himself marching into the front office with his resignation.

"Why, Mac, how can we do without you?" they'd say,
and he'd say, "Sorry, Mr. Clemens, I've got an offer from
Cal State. I just can't turn it down." What a day that
would be after eight long years in the boondocks. And it
was going to happen. It just had to!

Alex showed up for practice on Wednesday. His knee
was taped and he tried to show McAveety that he could
run, but it was obvious he was forcing it. A knee like his
was too vulnerable to a heavy tackle. If he jumped high
before being hit he could get away with it, but if the leg
were on the ground at the moment of impact, he'd be a
goner. McAveety kept him on the bench.

Brad and Alex avoided each other in a way that only
very close friends can do to hurt themselves. They said,
"Hi," and each went his own way thinking his own
thoughts, wondering how the impossible ever could have
happened. How that strong bond of loneliness that first
brought them together, the good times shared, the final

cement of admiration, their total commitment as friends, could have come apart.

As with Brad and Alex, tension over the game was building with all the players. So much was riding on this one. A winning season could make the difference in scholarships, in future plans, careers, the difference between a ticket to the outside world and a local dead-end job. Well, maybe not just one game. It was the three-year buildup of victories that was bringing statewide recognition. From here on, anything was possible.

Friday the whole thing boiled over in the shower room. Dutch and Brad were in adjoining showers, soaping themselves with the water off. And Dutch was shooting off his mouth as usual, this time aping McAveety's last-minute instructions.

"Okay, you jerks," he said, taking a stance like McAveety. "I want you cruds to get a good night's sleep, unnerstan'?"

There were shouts and a voice from a nearby shower, "Yessir, bossman, we gonna sleep good."

"You better," said Dutch. "And no takin' anything to bed with you, no sappin' them vital juices, get that?"

"Yeah, man," said a chorus of voices.

" 'Cause it says right there in the Good Book, that such goings-on before a game is an abomination. Right?"

"Right!" said the voices.

Dutch turned to Brad. "You go along, Mr. Quarterback?"

Brad smiled, went with it. "I go along."

"So if Miss Sally French was to come back and expose her gorgeous body, you got to say no." He grinned through the soapy lather. "Right?"

Brad didn't answer.

"What's the matter. Not funny?"

"Yeah," said Brad. "Not funny."

"What the hell," said Dutch. "You were her boy friend, what're you so touchy about?"

Brad swung his foot and caught Dutch a good kick in the ass. And then it was on. They started swinging and slipping on the floor. They grabbed hold of each other and pounded. And then they were wrestling, trying to hold onto each other's soapy body. The players gathered around. "Let 'em alone. Get back!"

But it was more comedy than drama. Dutch had soap in his eyes and couldn't see what he was doing. They rolled over, Dutch face down. Brad slid on top of him and got a lock on Dutch's wrist. Dutch was helpless. "Let go, you bastard!"

Brad whacked Dutch on the behind with his free arm. The players yelled encouragement.

"Dammit, I got soap in my eyes!" Dutch yelled.

Brad walloped him again.

"Cut it out, you jerk! Evans! Get this joker offa me!"

Evans came out of his shower. Alex, who had been in the last stall and heard it all, stepped in front of Evans. "Go finish your shower," Alex said.

"To hell with you," Evans said.

Alex hit him. And they were flailing away, the whole squad egging them on and Alex so mad and so full of adrenaline he was murdering the heavier Evans when a piercing whistle cut through the wild, yelling mess.

McAveety waded in, pulled them apart. The whistle was enough to get Brad off Dutch. They all stood there in silence like a bunch of delinquents caught in a bust.

"Get dressed, the lot of you," McAveety barked. "And go do twenty laps, no exceptions!"

There were groans, but they went back to their showers and washed off the soap.

McAveety stood over Dutch, who rolled over and sat up. "Somebody get me a towel, I can't see," Dutch complained.

There was laughter as the towel was thrown. Dutch wiped his eyes, looked up at McAveety. "I slipped, the floor was soapy." It sounded like a five year old talking to his mother. They all laughed openly as Dutch got to his feet. McAveety left the room, disgusted with them all.

Brad finished his shower. As he was leaving, he stopped in front of Alex, who was turning on his shower.

"Thanks," Brad said.

"For what?" asked Alex.

"For taking care of Evans."

Alex tried to smile, but his lip hùrt too much. " 'S okay," he said. "It was a pleasure."

Brad waved and moved on.

When Dutch left the shower room, there were amused smiles. But behind his back. Dutch was tough. Though not quite as tough as he used to be.

THE FINAL GAME with Jefferson drew a record crowd, including Congressman Van Harper, whose conspicuous presence assured coverage by more than the local press. The Fort Hanning band was seated in their special section with plenty of room for the big bass drum, which would celebrate every first down with wild tribal booms.

Excitement was building in the stands, people calling to each other, clenched fists raised to other clenched fists in pledges of victory, hand-printed banners appearing as patches of color in the bright autumn sunlight.

When Jefferson came on the field the visiting cheering section leaped to its feet in fervent response, throwing its small challenge across the field. Minutes later the Fort Hanning squad came out from under the stands and the unearthly roar sounded as if it were bouncing back off the mountains.

McAveety had sent them out with a prayer, and now he took his regular position just in front of the bench with his assistant coaches. His eye was on Brad, who was doing warm-up passes with his receivers. McAveety and Brad had agreed to keep to the ground in the first quarter to probe for a weak spot in the Jefferson defense. Short passes, okay, but save the big stuff.

As always, Brad had that tight, nervous feeling before the kickoff. He wished he were warming up with Alex. He could count on Alex. But Alex was sitting on the bench, flexing his knee, waiting, feeling he'd still be there at the end of the game, waiting.

Jefferson won the toss and elected to receive. The kick was too high. The Jefferson cornerback, fast and tough, took it on the twenty-five. Evans hit him on the thirty but couldn't hold on, the Jefferson man dodged, turned, swiveled, to the forty, the fifty, and then he was off and running with two blockers on either side. Dutch Graff came across the field like an enraged bull, but the Jefferson blockers converged and cut him down in the height of his fury. The Jefferson cornerback went over the line standing up.

There was crazy shouting in the Jefferson cheering section, but silence in the Fort Hanning stands as they made the point on conversion. Jefferson seven, Fort Hanning zero.

On the return kick, Fort Hanning ran it out to their thirty and as far as Brad was concerned the game was just beginning. His nervousness was gone. The early game play was correct. Three running plays gave them a first down on their forty. Two more, a short pass over the line, and another first down. The Fort Hanning bass drum woke up, boomed the cadence as the stands shouted, "Go, go go!"

Brad found a weakness in the short side of the Jefferson line and kept pounding it. A steady drive to the Jefferson fifteen brought a response from the Jefferson bench, a shift in formation, and two new players. With intuition and plain good sense, Brad hit the same spot, faking a pass and handing off to his flanker, who went through the hole and into the end zone for a touchdown. The conversion brought the stands to their feet in a long ovation.

And that's the way it was for the first half. In the second half, Jefferson intercepted a long bomb, ran it to the twenty-five, and kicked a field goal. Jefferson ten, Fort Hanning seven.

McAveety chewed on his dead cigar, watching his season trailing away with the clock. Between halves he had told Brad to take to the air, but the receivers weren't getting there. And the interception was almost a mortal blow.

In the final quarter, the Fort Hanning stands had settled into listless, silent watching. The cheerleaders jumped around trying to arouse them, but they were too spoiled by past successes to respond.

Brad kept his head, trying to calm his receivers, who were pressing too hard, outrunning the ball. Then, as the play went to the sidelines at midfield, he saw Alex warming up at the end of the stands. He's not going to put Alex in, thought Brad. The Jefferson defense has got to know about that knee; they'd go for him like a pack of wolves.

Coming back from a play Brad saw McAveety signal to Alex to return from the warm-up.

Jeezuz, he can't do it!

But Alex came to the bench and picked up his helmet.

Brad called time out.

McAveety clamped down on his cigar. What the hell was that kid doing?

Brad came to the sidelines, took off his helmet.

"What're you doing!" said McAveety angrily. "You gotta save your time-outs!"

Brad spoke low so the players wouldn't hear. "Prager's warming up. Are you putting him in?"

"You're damn right I'm putting him in."

"Well, I don't want him in."

"You don't want him!" McAveety couldn't believe it. He took Brad roughly by the arm and led him away from the benches. The players tried to ignore it, but they could see Brad and McAveety almost nose-to-nose, fighting in

low, tense words. Then suddenly McAveety pushed Brad
and Brad came back at him and McAveety swung a sharp
vicious backhand blow that caught Brad across the jaw
and sent him reeling. In seconds the assistant coaches
were over, took Brad by the arm, and led him to the sidelines. The whole thing took less than a minute. And at
least a thousand people saw it.

McAveety came over to Brad as if nothing had happened. "Keep it on the ground," he said, "till you get a
chance, then Red sixty-eight."

Brad nodded, time was resumed, and he went back on
the field with Alex. He called the running plays. The Jefferson defense tried to gang up on Alex and got a large
penalty for unnecessary roughness. In the huddle, Brad
wanted to reach out and pat Alex and say, "That's sucking
them in, Alex." But Brad said nothing. Yet the other
players felt it and they grinned, and suddenly there was
an undercurrent of hope, a revival of spirit. Guts, that's
what this guy had, bad knee and all. Brad felt very good
about his friend Alex.

First down on the Jefferson forty, three minutes to
play. Okay, it was the old college try, one for the Gipper,
and all that crap, but Brad was going to do it.

They were in the huddle. "Red sixty-eight, go on two."

They moved smartly to the line of scrimmage. The ball
was snapped. Brad ran back, well protected in the pocket.
There goes Alex down the sideline. Brad pumped a fake
to the tight end. In that fraction of an instant he thought
it out. He could throw the ball just a few feet long and
Alex would miss. And McAveety wouldn't have an undefeated season. McAveety's shiny record wouldn't be quite
so shiny. Just a few feet long and there goes McAveety's
record, he wouldn't be the Golden Boy heading for the
big time. McAveety would get his, but good!

All this went through Brad's head in that instant. He
had the power to cripple McAveety, not destroy him, but
bring him down, give him back that punch, fix the cheap

little bastard for risking a crippling injury to Alex to win himself a game.

But Brad threw a long, beautiful bomb right where Alex was going to be and Alex was there to make a spectacular catch and run it out into the end zone for the touchdown. Even though he'd wanted to, Brad couldn't throw it any other way.

The Fort Hanning defense held Jefferson till the clock ran out. McAveety had an undefeated season. But the Cal State scout who was up in the stands with McAveety's contract in his pocket had seen Brad get hit. A coach, whatever the provocation, does not hit one of his players.

When the scout got back to his motel, he tore up McAveety's contract.

IT WAS THE day before the Thanksgiving vacation and the whole English class was fidgety, wondering why Miss Dennis didn't let them go early. Brad watched the back of Kay's head as she bent over her notebook. He wondered what was going on inside that head. Maybe it was better if he didn't know. She had pointedly ignored him when she came into class with Jane Donnelly, the newest member of her group.

Brad winced inwardly, thinking of Jane Donnelly on that miserable night at Kelly's Place when they had found Alex. He could hear Jane saying, in that superbitch voice of hers, "Well hello, imagine finding you boys here."

Brad vaguely heard Miss Dennis say something about Kipling and the pride of empire. Kay was getting it all down. But he couldn't use her notes anymore, he'd have to start taking his own. He sighed heavily and opened his notebook.

"That's all for today," Miss Dennis said at last, smiling. She had let them off six minutes early.

The class cleared out as though she had called a fire drill. Brad didn't move. Why rush, he wasn't going anywhere. Last year this time it was all excitement, getting ready for the backpack with Alex. Well, there wouldn't be any trip this year, even though they'd planned it way back last summer.

He had promised his mother he'd be home tomorrow. She had planned something very special for Thanksgiving, she had said. He knew why. They were trying to patch things up, his mother and father, trying to look like a family again. It probably wouldn't work, but they wanted to give it a try.

Brad got up from his seat, stretched, turned to see Ellie also still sitting in her chair. She looked up from her notebook and smiled. "What did she say? Pride of Empire?"

"Yeah." He walked back to her seat. "Throw in 'white man's burden' if you want an A."

Ellie laughed. He sat down on the next chair, glanced at her notebook. "You get it all down?"

"I think so. You need a copy?"

He laughed. "Hey, you notice things, don't you?"

"I've never seen you take a note."

"I depend on Kay. Scratch that. I used to depend on Kay."

She looked toward the door, where Kay had left with the class. "I heard about that. I'm sorry."

"Yeah, me too. Kay's a good kid."

"Maybe after a while . . ."

"No, it's over. I think she's looking at fresher fields."

He glanced at her notebook. "Yeah, I guess I could read your handwriting."

She smiled. "You're welcome, any time." She closed the book, stood up. Brad got up. They walked out of the classroom and down the hall together.

"Home?" Brad asked.

"I guess so. But I'd really rather go anyplace else."

"The Food Factory," he said. "We could have something ghastly like a wheat-grass sandwich."

Ellie laughed. "I'd love it."

They walked to the parking lot and Brad took the bike off its stand.

"Do you know something unbelievable?" Ellie said. "I've never been on one of these things."

"This one's gentle as a kitten." He kicked it over and the bike came to life with a roar.

"Kitten?" she said nervously.

He laughed and threw his leg over the saddle. "Put the books between us and get on."

Ellie put her leg over the long black saddle.

"Now grab me around the waist."

Ellie did as she was told, holding on as if the end were near. He took off gently and wheeled out of the parking lot. Ellie held on tighter. He turned his head, smiled at her. "You'll like it once you catch on."

Ellie nodded, wondering if she would ever come out of it alive. But by the time they got to the Food Factory, she was wondering if Brad would ever invite her to ride again.

Chapter Twenty-two

KITTY WAS IN her room deciding on a dress for the Thanksgiving surprise. She wasn't really much of a cook and so the surprise was to be an elegant dinner at Le Petit Jardin. Just the three of them. She had ordered a special French wine for the major; she hoped he'd appreciate it.

Funny how she was thinking of Jim as the major. As if the marriage were over and she was referring to someone in the past. Yes, the major used to like that wine, she might say to the vague next gentleman, whomever he might be. Hold on, Kitty, this dinner is going to help patch things up, remember?

It wouldn't be easy to make the patch-up. She hadn't seen the major in more than a week; in one way, a relief. He'd been in the field on the testing range. She didn't know what kind of a mood he'd be in. When he'd gotten in late the night before she told him about Thanksgiving and all he said was, okay, and went to his room. Kitty threw several dresses on the bed for selection. No, it wasn't going to be easy.

Brad looked up from his copy of *Cycle World* to observe his father standing in the archway of the living room, dressed in his gray tweed suit, the Establishment three-button model he wore for special off-duty occasions.

He hadn't seen his father when he came in the night before. "Hi, Dad, how was home on the range?"

The major smiled thinly. "I survived."

"Good," Brad said, closing the magazine. "Mom ready?"

"Your mother is never ready," the major said as he came into the room. Brad noticed a copy of the *Fort Hanning Chronicle* under his arm. The major sat down, looked at his watch. "I think we can count on twenty minutes before your mother makes her appearance. We will, of course, be late twenty minutes at the restaurant."

"Yes, sir," Brad said, and reopened the copy of *Cycle World*.

After a minute or so he became aware that the major was rattling the paper more than necessary.

"Bradford . . ."

Brad looked up. "Yes, sir?"

"I've been catching up on the news." He held up the paper. "I've been reading about the game on Saturday. You evidently acquitted yourself nobly."

"Thanks," said Brad, "but we barely got out of that one alive. They almost clobbered us."

"Our local sportswriter didn't mention that."

"No, sir." Brad smiled. "He wouldn't."

"He did, though, go on at great length about the remarkable passing combination of Stevens and Prager."

"Yes, sir, he did," Brad said with a sigh. "I read it. Really gushy stuff."

"Yes, unfortunately gushy. I could have done without the Damon and Pythias angle."

"Me, too," said Brad. "That was good for a lot of laughs in the locker room."

"I imagine so," said the major dryly.

"But what the hell, you can't tell them how to write their newspaper."

"Can't you?"

"Well, no, sir." He looked at his father closely. "You don't think I had anything to do with that gush?"

"The writer seemed to know a lot about you and Alex."

"Well sure, we've been throwing footballs for three years in this town, maybe it's time they noticed."

"Don't be flippant, Bradford."

"I'm not being flippant, sir, I'm just saying it's no secret that I pass the ball to Alex on certain plays."

"It is also no secret that he is your best friend."

Brad was getting very angry. "He was my friend. You ordered me to drop him. I did drop him. What more do you want?"

The major slapped his paper against the arm of the chair. "I want some respect!"

Brad jumped up. "You've got respect! Why don't you want something else! Like love or friendship, or anything else!"

"Sit down, Bradford."

"My God, Dad, come off the drill field for once!"

"And don't use profane language at me. You're talking to your father."

"No, sir, I'm talking to my commanding officer. If you were my father, you'd understand about me and Alex just the way Mr. Prager understands."

"I know what Alex is, that's all I need to know."

"No, sir, you need to know a lot more! You need to know about me, how I feel!"

"I think you'd better go to your room, Bradford."

"Alex is the only real friend I ever had. I don't care what else he is, he's my friend. I never had time to make a friend before, with us hopping from post to post."

The major's voice grew tougher. "Go to your room, Bradford. Right now."

"No, sir, I am not going to my room."

The major clenched his fists. "That's an order, Bradford."

Brad just stood there soldier-like, ramrod straight, his eyes unafraid.

The major looked at his son, measuring, calculating. He stared for a long moment, then abruptly left the room. Brad could hear him go up the stairs and slam the door of his bedroom.

Brad took a deep breath. He walked to the hall closet and got out his backpack. He went into the kitchen and began filling his pack with groceries. With a grim smile, he picked up a can of cranberries, chucked it into the pack. After all, it *was* Thanksgiving.

HE WALKED FAST, working out his anger on the narrow blacktop road that led out of town into the mountains. Mug bounded ahead sniffing the fenceposts, racing back, barking, making sure that they were really on their way.

Six miles later, Brad climbed the fence and took the familiar trail up the Saddle Back Ridge. As he climbed, slogging along steadily, breathing easily, the anger began to wash away, to lose itself in the serenity of the tall trees, the small hum of insects, the rustle of unseen ground birds feeding in the underbrush.

He called to Mug and threw him a stick. Mug brought it back and Brad grabbed hold. They pulled and whirled around. Mug growled fiercely and Brad laughed, fighting, pulling the big dog right off his feet. But Mug held on and won the battle, racing ahead up toward the ridge with the stick in his mouth.

Brad smiled, hunched up his pack, and hit the trail. The climb was steeper now, but he hardly seemed to feel it. He was part of all that was going on in these woods, no need to think, only to get to the top of the ridge.

At the top he stopped for the first time. He could see endless hills and mountains, green touched with autumn yellow. Fort Hanning was hidden down there to the east. Nothing broke in on the sense of untouched wilderness.

Now he walked more slowly down the trail. He could hear Mug far ahead, barking. It wasn't Mug's I-found-a-rabbit bark, but more joyful, very excited. Brad moved a little faster. Mug came racing up the trail, stopped fifty yards ahead, barked, danced around, then dashed back down the trail.

Brad continued down and rounded a slight bend in the

trail. Alex standing there, leaning over and patting Mug.

Alex looked up and smiled.

Brad walked slowly toward him.

"Hi," said Alex.

"Hi," Brad said, smiling. "Where you headed?"

"Chinese Camp."

"Want company?"

"Sure thing," Alex said.

"Okay." Brad turned to Mug. "Go get 'em, Mug!"

Mug raced ahead on the trail.

Brad and Alex walked side by side. Brad set the pace the way they used to do it, steady, in measured, pleasant cadence.

There wasn't a need to talk right now. That they were there, together, said enough. And each was thinking that it wasn't an accident, being there. It was, in itself, a way of saying what wouldn't have been easy to put into words.

They moved on, heading into the mountain toward Chinese Camp. They glanced at each other now and then, feeling the old closeness, the wordless bond of friendship.

They camped early at the foot of a large rock cliff. When Mug was fed and the fire going well, they sat down with a cup of coffee, each waiting for the other to speak. But the silence between them was not awkward or hesitant, just comforting. They looked into the fire, thinking back, each remembering other times and knowing now, for sure, that this was not the end of those times, but only another beginning.

ABOUT THE AUTHORS

ANNE SNYDER, in addition to writing books and educational material, is active in the field of television. She is also a teacher of creative writing and has taught at Valley College, Pierce College, and University of California, Northridge. Her novel, FIRST STEP, published by Signet in paperback, was a winner of the Friends of American Writers Award. Her novels, MY NAME IS DAVY—I'M AN ALCOHOLIC and GOODBYE, PAPER DOLL, are also published by Signet. She and her husband live in Woodland Hills, California.

LOUIS PELLETIER, co-author of COUNTER PLAY, includes among his many TV credits such shows as GENERAL ELECTRIC THEATER, HAWAIIAN EYE and THE LOVE BOAT. Long associated with Walt Disney Studios, he scripted such movies as BIG RED, THOSE CALLOWAYS, and THE HORSE IN THE GREY FLANNEL SUIT. A resident of Pacific Palisades, Pelletier has taught screenwriting at University of California, Northridge, and University of California, Riverside.